Paddy And
The Wizard

Monique McCracken

PublishAmerica

Baltimore

First printing

ISBN: 1-59286-141-5
PUBLISHED BY PUBLISHAMERICA BOOK
PUBLISHERS
www.publishamerica.com
Baltimore

Printed in the United States of America

Chapter One

Barefooted Paddy ran happily over the hot sand.

His long skinny legs stopped bouncing as he watched a black cloud appearing in the perfectly blue sky. In his sudden halt, his pointed leather hat fell onto the sand. Long strings of pale hair tossed in the wind and rushed forward over his bright green eyes. The cloud lingered for a few seconds and just as suddenly vanished.

"Wow, what's that?" whispered Paddy.

His dog Tiger looked up at the cloud and growled.

"Don't be in such a hurry, man," said his friend, Daryl, following puffing, dragging his short, stubby legs. He had his dirty red baseball cap turned backward with dark wet hair dripping in the back. At that moment, his mischievous blue eyes had lost their sparkle. He didn't like to be left behind.

"Did you see that?" asked Paddy.

"What?" Daryl answered grumpily.

"The black cloud."

"There is no cloud in the sky," Daryl said with a chuckle of superiority.

Paddy dropped his running shoes and splashed into the incoming surf to join Tiger. "Never mind," he replied.

The end of the holidays was close. With the boys gone, the beautiful Roshgull Peninsula in the North West of Ireland would return to its pristine calm.

Daryl, all sweaty, fell heavily into the water to cool off. Blue T-shirts and denim shorts sticking to their bodies, the boys romped in the surf with Tiger barking as he joined them in the friendly fight.

"A dark cloud!" snickered Daryl, then, grinning wickedly, he said, "Let's climb the Melmore Head."

"No! Mom doesn't approve of us going up there." Paddy threw a handful of wet sand at Daryl.

"Come on, don't be a chicken! Be a good sport, man."

Paddy put on his running shoes, brushed the sand off his wet legs, licked his lips and shyly looked at the big rock. It was mighty high.

"All right, enough fuss, man. Let's go!" Daryl ran.

The climb under the August sun was not pleasant. They slipped, scratched hands and knees. More than once, Paddy's heart was ready to fly out of his chest.

Tiger watched them from the top, barking encouragingly. Daryl's long hair dripped water onto his back and forehead. Unlike his friend, Paddy hadn't turned into a dribbling fountain. He had arrived first at the summit and sat rubbing his knees. Daryl had dropped back.

"We made it, Daryl."

Daryl collapsed behind him. Without a word he threw his red baseball cap on the ground and furiously pulled off his wet T-shirt.

Paddy waited for Daryl to get over his grumpiness. Arms around his knobby knees, he watched the waves below crashing into the big rocks with a muffled sound. The seagulls in the sky wheeled and squawked. Sadly, Paddy remembered his dad, who died at sea, two summers ago, during a fishing party off the New England coast, when he was ten. They lived then in Boston where his Dad met his Mom and married her. As a family they had come every summer to Ireland, place of birth of his parents.

Daryl was still brooding; he couldn't stand not being always first.

"Hey, Daryl, are you going to nurse your scratches all afternoon?"

"Nope."

"Good! Now you have us up here, what are you suggesting we should do?" Paddy jackknifed his long legs, turned around, propped his chin on his scratched knees. "Mom won't like these knees, Daryl."

"We can say we tumbled on the rocks. Close enough to the truth, no?"

"I guess so. "

"How come you are scared of everything, man?" Daryl retorted, jumping up, and then finding a perfect, round stone. With a powerful swing of his stubby right leg, he kicked it toward the ocean.

"Wow! That was a mighty kick, man."

Daryl smiled. No one in the village had his strength to kick a football. Paddy's joy was running. Even Daryl couldn't beat him.

"We have a long way to walk down, man," said Paddy. Tiger barked in approval.

"OK, boy, we go. You don't need to be so blaring," Daryl said with a chuckle.

Carefully, they picked their way down. Tiger sat on his tail and barked his head off! They ignored him and, arrived at a dead end, a large cave.

"This isn't the way we came up before!" whispered Paddy fearfully

"Nope, Tiger told us that all along. Let's explore a little."

"Don't like this," mumbled Paddy.

"Come on. Have a little sense of adventure, man."

They walked for a while into a winding tunnel. Tiger joined them, and Paddy said apprehensively, "We have gone far enough Daryl. Let's return, it's dark and spooky down here."

Just then a shaft of light appeared with a weirdly dressed man, wearing green skin-tight pants and a white satin tunic held by a gold leather belt. From his shoulders hung a long grey cape. His high brown leather boots reached almost to his knees. A green pointed hat (Like mine, noted Paddy) covered his long silvery hair. The light disappeared, and the man stayed. Tiger, wagging his tail, went to him as if recognizing a friend. Startled, Paddy gulped and asked,

"Who are you?"

"I am a magician from the Elfic Realm."

Daryl could only look, his mouth hanging open.

Paddy whispered, "The man must be a lunatic living in the cave."

"There is no such thing as the Elfic Realm and magicians are in circuses," cried Daryl taking off.

Paddy, suddenly terrified, scooted away in the dark and in his flight passed Daryl.

"Wait, boys! Wait! I have wonderful stories to tell you."

Paddy came to a sudden halt. He loved stories, especially Irish tales. Daryl, arriving at full speed behind, bumped into him, and both of them tumbled onto the dirt. Quickly Daryl picked himself up, and ran screaming, "Let's get away from here, man!"

Paddy scrambled up and dashed away, leaving Daryl behind. The man ran with Tiger now right beside Paddy, and the mouth of the cave wasn't coming any closer.

"I can tell you Magic stories from my realm."

"And where is that?" asked Paddy.

"Beyond the rainbow."

"What?" Paddy was almost sick with fear.

"The man is nuts!" puffed Daryl from the rear.

* * *

In the darkness the man shone again, and vanished. The boys, caught in the same light, found themselves running on the sandy beach. Above his panting mouth, Daryl's blue eyes were round as saucers. "How did we get here?" Daryl said, puffing.

"Don't know! Better not talk about this to Mom."

"What a shocker."

They took the path going up through the rolling hills. Short of breath, they arrived at the cottage. Anxiety stung Paddy. His mother was going to ask questions about their afternoon. He wiped his sweaty brows, cracked the door, and peeked inside. No one was there. The note on the kitchen table read, "I am going to the market to get lobsters for supper."

They went outside to play a game of kick the can. Tiger joined in. When Tara arrived, the excitement was great and noisy. She cried a joyous "Hi, guys!"

"Hi, Mom!" replied Paddy.

After supper the boys sat outside on the stone bench with Tiger at Paddy's feet and quietly talked about their experience.

A few days later Tara packed their bags. Summer was over. Now school awaited them.

* * *

Paddy and Daryl, skipping on their skateboards, were on their way to school, talking and laughing about their holidays. Daryl, skeptical about the encounter in the cave, laughing said, "You like the fantastic, man!"

"But how do you explain the fact that we found ourselves on the beach at the foot of the rock?" asked Paddy.

"Yes, bizarre. Don't know, and don't care!" Daryl shrugged grumpily.

They parked their boards against the wall in the schoolyard. It was an exciting day, because during recess the kids noisily recounted their summer fun.

Paddy with a grimace gathered his new books, many more than the year before, stuffed them into his shoulder bag and left the yard on his skateboard. Daryl was busy comparing his prowess with his chums.

Chapter 2

Tara's cottage was on a paved road in a village, a short bike ride from Donegal. To the delight of Paddy and his friends, the village had a general mercantile stuffed with cookies, candies and peanuts, beside it was the notion store, carrying shining satin, soft velvet, lace and ribbons of every color, to the delight of the girls. The junk store on Main Street was full of treasures for the boys. Paddy, spent lots of time there looking for mysterious objects. The two friends homes were almost next door to each other and not far from the high cliffs rounding the coast. Since his father's death, Paddy, to escape from reality, and his Mom, had taken to walking the dusty trail going up to the cliffs.

Next day, after school, Paddy asked Daryl to come along with him to the cliffs, "Perhaps the strange man will come," said Paddy.

"Nope. Thanks. That man, in my books, never existed. Come on, man, be realistic." Daryl went back to bickering with his friends.

Disappointed Paddy left. A nippy September breeze ruffled his hair. Shivering, he zipped up his windbreaker and pushed hard on his pointed hat. When he arrived at the top of the cliffs, he sat at his favorite place and watched the waves rolling their white caps from the horizon.

Then in a ray of light appeared the man saying, "Hello, Paddy. I will come back to tell you the promised stories." And in a burst of light, he was gone.

"Wow! How did he do that?" Excited, he dashed for Daryl's home and bolted into the yard shouting,

"Daryl, Daryl, I have something important to tell you! The man returned and promised to tell me stories!"

"What! That's a joke, man! You are a good story teller yourself."

Daryl slapped Paddy's back.

"But, it's true!"

Hurt, Paddy walked home to the stable. Baltazar, the little donkey, greeted him with joyous brays. Tiger arrived with puffs of dirt flying behind him,

"Hi, guys! Come Tiger, let's have a glass of milk." Paddy pushed the kitchen door. Tara was preparing the evening meal. "Hi, Mom, Tiger and I would like some milk." Quietly, he poured a glass for himself and a bowl for Tiger. They went out and sat under the apple tree. Frustrated, he mumbled, "What a louse Daryl can be." Tiger barked.

"How come you understand everything, Tiger?"

That morning Paddy didn't see Daryl on the road. It was a dull day. Class over, he walked to the store and got some peanuts, smarties and a bunch of chocolate cookies. Munching away downcast, he dragged his feet to the cliffs kicking stones. As he arrived, he dropped his school bag on the ground, flopped on the dry grass, pulled out the smarties. A pang of anxiety churned his stomach. The man was there, facing the ocean like an eagle ready to soar. He said, "Hello, Paddy. Would you like to come into my realm?"

Paddy, curious and a bit scared, cried, "Yes! But, how did you know I was here?"

"Magician's tricks, boy."

"Aaah...."

"Give me your hand, and come into a Realm of wonders. Come to learn valor and courage."

Hesitantly, dry mouthed, Paddy held his hand up in mid-air. A tremor of fear ran through him. Then quickly he gave his hand.

* * *

In a flash, Paddy found himself on a knoll in a hazy forest full of frightening sounds. A small creature, dressed, in what looked like a burlap sac, greeted him. He was bald, with bat's ears and large slanted blue eyes shining on a dark yellow skin. His thin lips parted in a smile, showing white saw blade teeth. The little creature introduced himself as Woody, Djinn of the forest. Woody explained to Paddy, "We are in the domain of a wicked witch named Yerty, daughter of a king, whose kingdom lies at the foot of the Purple Mountains, days to the west. While growing up, Yerty's wickedness became so great that her father banished her from the kingdom. Since then, she hates her younger sister Lial."

Paddy, baffled, dropped on the moss watching the Djinn.

"The Witch plots her evil schemes, at the top of this tower, in The Forest of Shadows, which is where we are now. See, listen. She is confiding to her nasty servant."

Paddy with the Djinn's help, heard and saw the two women talking, "I wonder how to get rid of Lial?" the witch said.

Paddy, flabbergasted, asked, "How is this possible? How come I see and hear them?"

The Djinn said, "I gave you the gift of hearing all things and seeing from afar. Use it well."

"Never! I must get out of here, presto!" Paddy jumped to his feet.

"You are here to help. That is why Niko sent you," Woody replied harshly.

"No! That storyteller is crazy! I'll go home!" he cried angrily. "I won't go west or east! I- w- o- n-'t- go!"

Woody had vanished. "Where are you?" screamed Paddy in panic. Only the sinister whisper of the wind answered. Fear sat right in his stomach. Stunned, he stayed for a while, then picked himself up from the ground and left for the king's palace. The walk through the underbrush was hard and painful. He fell many times. Mumbling indignantly, "Shouldn't have put my hand in that man's hand. Daryl's right. I am crazy."

The thorns grabbed his windbreaker. Wretched, he fought them. Lonely for home, dead tired, he munched his cookies, crawled under a bush and fell asleep with the forest whispering around.

In his slumber he heard the witch saying to her servant "Go to my sister with a note asking for her help." Yerty cackled with joy. "She will come."

Paddy woke up. In his mind he saw the hag on her mule. Terrified he ran, and as he ran, he watched her arriving and presenting the matter to the young princess.

Her Nanny pleaded, "Don't go. Your sister is wicked! "

Paddy screamed, "Don't go, Lial. It's a trap!" Evidently, she couldn't hear him.

" I'll go!" replied Lial.

"All right, then, I will come with you."

Nanny Mirga, with a few magic words and a twist of her hand, whisked them to the tower. Yerty laughed with pleasure. Greeting her servant, she said, "Now, I am going to get rid of you for good, sister!"

Mirga desperately tried to wish them back to the castle, but none of her magic worked.

"My power is stronger than yours," laughed the witch. "All right, sister, what would you like to be? A monkey? A goat? Ah! A doe. That is you! What about you Mirga? The wise owl. That's it!"

Paddy in his mind saw Yerty's calling out spell after spell. Feathers flying everywhere, Mirga fought back, coming in and out of the spell.

* * *

Paddy saw Lial changed into a doe in the enchanted forest and Mirga perched on a tree flapping her wings furiously. Lial was asking, "Can you do something about it Mirga?

"Hooo, hooo, I have tried, dear."

Demoralized, Paddy continued, plodding through the evening fog. Then a whiff of smoke reached his nose. He followed the welcome smell to a bushman's hut and knocked at the door. The man and his wife were about to eat. And she served him a bowl of hot soup with bread and cheese. Paddy, meal over, left the good people.

Paddy's mind was set on returning to the knoll, with the hope of finding Woody and asking for his help to return home. Head down, he mumbled, "I shouldn't have embarked on such an adventure. What if I am trapped in this realm? I miss you, Mom. I am so scared."

Night had fallen and, completely exhausted, Paddy dropped to the ground and slept. A few hours later a voice woke him.

"Hooo, hooo, Who are you?" asked an owl perched upon a tree. Startled, Paddy jumped up and looked around.

"Where are you? My name is Paddy, a human boy. I came to help Princess Lial, but I don't know what to do! I was hoping to find Woody."

"Woody's not here. A human boy you said? Follow me."

Paddy didn't have time for questions. "Wait! Wait!" The owl flew away, Paddy scrambled to follow. After hours of running, they arrived in a green meadow where a young doe moved clumsily. Princess Lial was trying to adjust to walking on four legs. The owl perched herself on a branch.

Shyly, Paddy approached. "My name is Paddy, I came to help you, princess." Exhausted by his run, he dropped on the moss. For the longest time, they talked, trying to find a solution to the dilemma. Thirsty, the doe was attracted by the sound of a bubbling creek. She jumped up to reach the water. A frightened cry stopped her. "No! Don't Lial !"

"Why Mirga?"

"That water is evil," replied the owl.

Startled Paddy saw the brook begin to boil and red eyes in the clear water flashed angrily.

"Don't stay here," cried Paddy terrified.

Led by Mirga, they found another meadow. Now it was almost dark. A big tree, with boughs touching the ground, made a perfect shelter for the night. Mirga perched on a branch, watching. Paddy, exhausted, fell asleep.

The next morning, a yawning Paddy crawled out from under the boughs. He sat on a broken branch and pulled out a bag of cookies. Mirga, on a limb flapped her wings. The doe came and with tears in her voice asked. "What are we going to do?"

Paddy thoughtfully replied, "We must find the witch and trick her into restoring your human form."

They started out and soon came to a beautiful lake. The water was terribly inviting and they were so thirsty. But after the past experience, Paddy was scared! "Don't go Lial, I feel evil. Something's wrong here," he said.

"No, look at the water, it is so clear," she replied. Paddy stayed close behind her, then she put her dainty hooves into the water.

"No!" Cried Paddy.

Too late! The boy just had time to catch one hind hoof as Lial was pulled into the lake.

Chapter 3

Lial shrieked with terror. She was falling into a bottomless pit. Paddy lost his grip just before the incredible voyage ended in a dark cave dimly lit by two resin torches. Paddy had dropped a few meters behind her.

A tall ugly man, in a red cape, stood before Lial who had returned to her human form. He laughed, proud of how he had lured her into his trap, "I am Lord Wargo, Master of all the lakes, brooks and waters of the Enchanted Forest. Come girl, let's move." A thin bony hand grabbed Lial, and pulled her toward a dark slimy tunnel lit by dingy smoky torches. Fear gripped Paddy's heart. Shaking with fear he followed in the dark. Several times Lial stumbled. Shadows crept along the walls At last, the sorcerer arrived in front of a large door. Paddy quickly hid himself.

The sorcerer made a strange gesture. With the help of Woody's, gift Paddy's mind followed him, as the door silently opened into a sinister room, lit by a single candelabra holding a huge red candle, dripping a large pool of red wax like blood on the floor. The door closed.

"What a spooky place," whispered Paddy. At the far end of the sinister chamber was a massive black and red seat with a high back. Red drapes fell on each side, and from behind them appeared a strange hooded creature dressed in a dark brown cloak. It was half bent and dragging a crippled leg. The thing oozed into the room and bowed to the ground in fear.

"Take her away! Escort the girl to her chamber."

No sound escaped the creature's mouth. She grabbed Lial's dress, and pulled the shocked girl. As the door opened, Paddy waiting in the shadows, followed down the poorly lit corridor. They stopped and the creature opened a door, brutally pushed Lial inside, and left.

In the dark hall Paddy waited. Then magically the door opened. Cautiously he entered. A wee torch lit the room. The furniture consisted of a bed, armchair, and a table covered with a shawl touching the floor. Lial was stunned when she saw Paddy. Aghast, she whispered, "You, here !"

"Yes, as you went down, I grabbed your hind leg and followed you."

"How come the door opened to let you in?"

Puzzled, Paddy shrugged. "Don't know! Hush."

Paddy quickly crawled under the table and pulled the shawl behind him. A smiling Lady entered, "My name is Zelda, and like yourself I am a prisoner of Wargo," she said, "If his plot succeeds the Enchanted Forest will be lost forever."

"What plot?" asked Lial.

"Wargo is to marry you. That's the key to his success."

"What, marry me!" She screamed terrified.

"Hush girl. He can't accomplish his horrible plans without you. You can come out now, Paddy"

Paddy crawled out from his hiding place.

"Hello, Paddy. I opened Lial's door for you. Listen, there is a way to get free of Wargo. A pair of Diamond Slippers is hidden at the bottom of a lake. Only he can retrieved the slippers. I will trick him to get them. Lial, you must wear the slippers night and day for three months. At the end of the three months, Paddy will break the slippers with the Magic Hammer. Only a human boy by crushing the Diamond Slippers can defeat the sorcerer. That is why you are here, Paddy."

"Where is this hammer?" asked Paddy fearfully.

"On the top of a rock standing in the middle of a Lake, guarded by a giant swordfish, one of Wargo's creatures. Here, Paddy, is a magic ring. It will make you and Lial both invisible when you hold her hand. Now come with me." They went cautiously in the tunnels, when arriving at a fork, the Fairy stopped. "This is the way to Mirador Lake. Paddy, you go to your right."

"Yes, ma'am." Paddy's voice was faint.

They returned to Lial's cell. Zelda took from her pocket a little vial and said, "Drink this, it is a magic herb, Lial. You will look like death itself. The sorcerer is busy with the preparations for the wedding tomorrow. That is why I give you the magic herb to drink now."

Paddy watched Lial swallow the potion and saw her turn a pale ghostly green. She lay on the bed and Zelda quietly left the room. Paddy crawled under the table to hide and found the fairy had provided a soft mattress, a pillow and a warm comforter. Exhausted he fell asleep. With the help of his magic gift, Paddy in his slumber heard and saw Wargo pacing restlessly, muttering, "tomorrow I will be the Lord and Master of the Enchanted Forest. I will crush them all!" With a terrible laugh, he waved his hand, and one of his creatures appeared. "Get the girl, hurry!.."

The thing, hobbling, left and a few minutes later returned. He entered the room crawling on his knees. Sore afraid, he whispered, "Master, the girl is very sick."

"What!"

The Sorcerer ran out, lights flashed from his eyes! He slammed the door and like a tornado arrived at Lial's cell and stopped sharp at the door!

Lial, green as a ghost, had perspiration running in rivulets along her cheeks, and large black circles around her eyes. Her chest whistled as she labored to breathe.

"What is the matter? Get Zelda," Wargo screamed to his creature.

Zelda's trick had worked. A few minutes later she arrived. "You sent for me, My Lord?"

"Yes. See what's wrong with this girl."

Under the table Paddy trembled with fear. What if the sorcerer discovered him? No, the fairy must have shielded him.

Zelda approached and touched Lial. She jumped back as if a snake had bitten her.

"What's the matter, woman?"

"She is under a terrible spell, My Lord."

"What! What spell? Who did it?" He screamed.

"Probably Brina, Genie of the mountain. She does not approve of your marriage"

"How outrageous! How dare she!" He yelled in rage.

"There is a way to defeat her, My Lord."

"Speak, woman."

"At the bottom of the lake Mirador you have a pair of Diamond Slippers."

"What about them? How do you know it?"

"Fairies know almost everything, My Lord. My Lord must get the slippers. Lial will wear them night and day for three months. During that time you must not see her, or she will die." In furor, he left the room.

"I must follow him in my mind," mumbled Paddy. Then he saw the sorcerer, head resting on a fist, sat on his throne talking to himself. "How can I cancel that terrible spell? I don't want to take the Slippers out of Mirador's lake. The powerful fairy I tricked inside the Slippers is dangerous! If I don't get them, the girl dies. Her death will ruin all my plans."

Paddy, terrified, watched him. The more the sorcerer thought, the more he boiled with rage. His face became purple; lightning flashed in his eyes, then he left in a crash of fire and smoke. Paddy in his mind followed. Like a tornado, he arrived at the lake. With one furious gesture, he brought the Slippers out of the water into his right hand, and quickly closed his claws upon them.

Then laughing sardonically he said, "How are you Star-Moon? Don't think of escaping just because I am taking you out of the lake. No way, my dear! You are here for a special purpose and when it's over, it's back into the water with you."

In a cloud of smoke he vanished. Paddy was still following him in his mind. Wargo, entered like a whirlwind into Lial's room. Paddy relaxed.

"I have the Slippers!" he shouted to the Fairy.

"Good! My Lord, now you must to put them on her feet."

"What!" he screamed, backing up. With disgust he did it and turned to leave. Zelda said, "No one comes into her room for three months, Lord Wargo, only myself."

With flames of rage in his eyes he dashed outside slamming the door. The Fairy moved her hands, colour came back to Lial's cheeks. "How do you feel?"

"Wonderful! I could see and hear everything. It was actually funny.
"

Paddy crawled out from under the table, and looked at the Slippers. He whistled and recounted what he saw in his mind at the lake. "What a jerk! " Suddenly his stomach growled. "Gosh, I am starved!"

"Me. too," uttered Lial.

"Don't forget, you must not take the Slippers off. I will provide food, games, and books. It will be three long months."

After their meal, Paddy went under the table. Longingly he thought about his mom and Tiger and fell asleep.

Chapter 4

Three months had passed. Zelda came to the children and said, "Soon Wargo will come to claim you. Let's not waste any time. Don't remove those slippers until Paddy is in possession of the magic hammer. Then quickly take them off, Paddy must smash them in one blow."

Paddy shivered as he quietly opened the door. A heavy silence mixed with a musty stink hung in the hall. Teeth chattering, he took the route followed by Lial.

Although the Slippers shone in the darkness with a light that only they could perceive, it was still hard to see the way. More than once they beat a fast retreat into a corner to avoid being discovered . At last they arrived at the big fork. Paddy whispered, "Oh boy! Which way? Don't remember! Do you?"

"No."

Then he heard the Fairy, "To the right."

For what seemed to be hours. they walked, and then Paddy saw lying in the middle of a cave, a huge sleeping thing. Fear, took hold of him. Sweat on his forehead, teeth clenched, he approached, ready to put on the ring of invisibility. A gentle voice spoke,

"Don't be afraid, children."

Terrified, they shrank back.

The voice, continued, "I am Zelda's friend. My name is Tulca. I will take you to the Magic Hammer. Climb upon my back." The voice belonged to a gigantic salamander.

Trying to be brave, Paddy asked, " I presume you know about our quest too?"

"Yes, I do. I was expecting you."

Paddy helped Lial up. Magically, a soft seat had been provided.

They traveled quickly. There in the center of the lake was the big rock.

"I am a good swimmer," said Paddy shaking with fear.

"Hush, boy. I will. If you were to put your feet in that water the swordfish would cut you to pieces. It's powerless against me. My hide is too thick."

Paddy helped Lial to the ground and watched the salamander ease herself into the water. She didn't make a single ripple. At the bottom of the lake the swordfish, with a powerful swing of its tail rose to the surface and sped toward the big lizard. Quickly Tulca turned and faced him. The swordfish's red beady eyes stared angrily at Tulca. In one long glide it attacked. She darted sideways and it missed. Water churned. Paddy realized that the only way Tulca had to end this was to destroy the sword. As if Tulca had read Paddy's thought, with her powerful jaws she snapped it at the base of the fish's nose. Defenseless, the swordfish dove into the depths of the lake. Tulca approached the rock, took the Magic Hammer into her mouth, and quickly swam back to shore.

Lial dropped the slippers on the ground. Paddy, smashed them in a single blow. Hundreds of stars filled the cave. A violent wind rose up sucking all the water from the lake. Horrible howling chilled Paddy's bones. Flames danced everywhere. (Monique, I like this paragraph very much!)

" Incredible! We defeated the Sorcerer!" cried Paddy.

They were outside by the lake where months ago both had been trapped. The salamander was gone. An Elf and a beautiful Fairy dressed in millions of stars smiled at him.

"Who are you ?" asked Paddy, stupefied . "Where is Tulca?"

"I am Tulca," said the Elf. "When the sorcerer trapped Star-Moon, he trapped me at the same time and turned me into a salamander. and locked me in the caves. Star-Moon is the Fairy of stars and moon. You, Paddy and Lial, were the only ones who could free us. Zelda had put into the mind of Lial's wicked sister the idea of tricking her in the Enchanted Forest."

"But how did I get into the quest?" asked Paddy.

Star-Moon explained. "We needed you, a human child, to crush the Diamond slippers. With the help of Niko the Wizard you came."

The Fairy Zelda arrived to transport them to King Umira's palace where Mirga waited.

Yerty and her servant were turned into beasts of burden by Star-Moon. They were to stay like that until they repented of their evil ways. It is said, that even to this day, their nastiness is so great that their masters have a hard time trying to cope with them.

For weeks, the kingdom of the Enchanted Forest celebrated their freedom and the return of their King, King Umira.

But a black cloud hovered above the realm. Wargo was still alive.

* * *

Dazed, Paddy looked around and shook his head. He was on the cliffs. Sheepishly, Paddy said to the man, "Sorry, I guess I fell asleep. What a dream!"

The man smiled.

Paddy, his fear forgotten, mumbled angrily, "I would have liked to fight that terrible Wargo." His face was inflamed by his desire for justice, and his eyes, shining with anger, were now a deep green.

"I am sure you would have fought bravely. I won't see you tomorrow, my young hero. You have the soul of a Knight."

"Really? " Paddy excited, sprang to his feet and left running singing heartily, "I have the soul of a Knight! At least in my dreams, " he said with a chuckle.

On his way home he bumped into Daryl, head swinging, with his Walkman plugged into his ears.

Gleefully. Paddy shouted at him, "Glad to see you," and he continued his happy song, skipping on the road. "I have the soul of a Knight! I have the soul of a Knight !"

Daryl ran after him laughing. "What's that? You are crazy! You mostly have the soul of a chicken, he said with his mouth full of jellybeans.

"I am not crazy. I am happy! Well, maybe I am a chicken, but today I am a knight with a magic sword fighting evil." Seeing Daryl's face Paddy said, "Come take your sword, O evil one. We will fight to the death !" Chuckling, Paddy hopped around Daryl.

"I honestly think you are crazy, Paddy."

They arrived at Paddy's house. Tiger, hearing the laughter, came to the gate and barked

Tara from the shed asked curiously, "What's all that noise about boys?"

"Don't know, Ma'am. Paddy shouts to the wind that he has the soul of a Knight, and then he challenges me to a duel. I think he cracked at the top."

"Why ? It's better to think you are a Knight, than a tramp.

Now, both of you settle down. Help me pile this load of wood in the wood shed, and then come in for a piece of pie."

"Wow! Yes, Mom. Yes, Ma'am," they replied in unison.

"A knight!" chuckled Daryl.

The chores finished, they ran to the house to eat the promised pie. Tiger put his head on Paddy's lap waiting for his share. Lots of chuckling and teasing from Daryl assailed Paddy. "A knight!" He puffed behind his hand. Their pie finished, they moved in front of the TV to watch "Superman", a favourite of theirs.

Daryl left. Paddy thought about what his friend had said of him...a chicken heart. He sighed. Daryl was right. He was not much of a hero, and even less a knight.

Next morning, Paddy dilly-dallied in his room. He was not in any great hurry to leave knowing only too well that Daryl would tell the boys about his claim to Knighthood. What a day it will be, he sighed.

"Hurry up, Paddy! You are late," called Tara.

Paddy dragged himself downstairs. "I am not feeling well, Mom."

"I know." She smiled, ruffling his hair gently. "I don't understand what came over you last night to tell Daryl, especially Daryl, that you had the soul of a Knight. But remember, a Knight wouldn't balk over unimportant things. He would charge on his steed and face the music. Now, have your breakfast, brave knight ."

Wholeheartedly Paddy attacked his bowl of cereal. Tiger's eyes watched every spoonful going into his mouth, waiting patiently for the leftovers.

As he left, Tara said from the door. "Remember, you are fearless. Smile and go."

"You are wonderful, Mom. Bye!" He walked away head up.

The day went as Paddy expected. Thanks to Daryl, he was the laughingstock of the school. He remembered what his mom said and smiled. Then, the boys stopped teasing.

When the bell rang, Paddy left and didn't run. He mumbled, "I "have to be more careful from now on about what I say to Daryl." However, he was happy. For the first time he had faced the music.

"Bye, Daryl. Come with me to the cliffs?"

"Nope, thanks for asking. I leave that to you ...dreamer! Maybe one day. Okay?"

Paddy, chuckling, swung his school bag on his shoulders and left. When he arrived, the man was not yet there. Quietly, he sat on the grass with his chin resting on his bent knees and his arms around his legs. "I conquered my fear, and Daryl promised, maybe..., to come along. It was a good day."

Satisfied, he listened to the soft beat of the ocean on the rocks below, and watched the endless rolling silvery waves coming toward the cliffs. "Wow! It's late!" he jumped to his feet and grabbed his bag.

His mother waited at the gate. "Where were you? I saw Daryl and asked him if he had seen you? Nope, was his answer."

Paddy went to the house and changed clothes for his chores. He loved taking care of Balthazar. The little donkey was always anxious to please. Chores finished, he and Tiger trotted to the old stone well and slumped beneath the apple tree.

"Sit, boy. I will tell you the dream I dreamed of Princess Lial and the human boy." The dog barked and barked! Tara, out in the garden, asked, "What's the matter with Tiger?"

"Nothing. Mom, Daryl and I will be on the road with our skateboards. Okay?"

"Don't be late for supper."

27

Paddy went to get Daryl, and they had a good race. Then Daryl stopped, tuned around and said, "Hey, man, look, we are being watched from behind the bush."

"You are cuckoo. No one's there. Bye!" Paddy dashed to the garden gate.

Supper finished, and his homework done, Paddy climbed upstairs. His head was too full of dreams to read or watch TV or surf the net. He went to sleep.

* * *

The next morning Paddy, at the garden gate , heard a real commotion. Daryl appeared, bolting down the road, his legs almost around his neck. Never had Paddy seen his friend move so fast. His father, milk dripping down his face and shirt, yelling in rage, followed with a stick in his hand.

"Just let me catch you, boy!"

"Wow ! Now what has he done this time?" Paddy left for school. Then he met Daryl's father coming back. The man red-faced and puffing was mumbling angrily to himself. Seeing Paddy, he shouted, "Tell Daryl he's not gaining anything by waiting. I will catch him sooner or latter." Menacingly he raised his stick.

"Yes, sir."

Later, from behind a bush came a, " ...psst.. psst... "

"All right Daryl, your father's gone. Oh boy! What have you done to make him so mad ?"

Daryl, his red cap all crooked, stretched his neck, and looked fearfully around. Then, chuckling, he said, "To poke my sister, I made a long stick with a sharp nail at the end. This morning, I decided to try it on Rosy, but I didn't see Dad milking her."

"What! Are you nuts Daryl ? On the cow !"

"It was funny ! She kicked Dad's stool. He fell head first into the bucket full of milk. When he pulled it off his head, I ran."

"No wonder the man wants to kill you!" Paddy was laughing.

"He hasn't caught me yet," chuckled Daryl.

"No? You are wrong. What about tonight, when you come home? By the way, your Dad asked me to tell you... that you were not gaining anything by waiting."

Daryl's joy fell flat. "What am I going to do ?" he whimpered.

"Ah, that, man, you should have thought about before."

"But I didn't see Dad! "

The school day was over. Paddy gave Daryl a slap on the back. All day Daryl's spirits had been low. The idea of his father waiting for him at home had made him restless. He certainly didn't give a hoot about what was being taught concerning the English-Irish battle. That was a mistake. During recess he had to write on the black board fifty times, ".I will listen to the teacher."

"Listen, man, go to your Dad. Tell him you are sorry, and from now on, you will behave."

"Won't work. Don't know if I will behave."

"Well, then, what can I say ?"

A dejected Daryl left.

Paddy watched him going away, and shouted, "Think about what I said man. Good luck!"

The wind was blowing, and the big waves crashed at the bottom of the cliffs with a dull boom. The seagulls squawked, enjoying the challenge the wind offered.

Paddy pulled his bag off his shoulders and sat and zipped up his windbreaker. With a sweep of his hand, he brushed the hair out of his eyes to look up at the old man, who had arrived.

"I am sorry, Paddy. Today, I cannot stay." He quietly departed in a shaft of light.

"Wow!" Paddy grabbed his bag, tossed it on his shoulder and left. On his way home, he had the uneasy feeling that he was watched. Paddy thought, "Daryl mentioned that a few days ago. But why? By whom?" Shivers ran along his back, and goose bumps raised his hairs.

Chapter 5

Tara impatiently waited for him at the garden gate with Tiger. "Come on, Paddy. Hurry up. Tell me what you have done with my new rolling pin."

"Haven't touched it, Mom." he replied shaking his head.

"How do you expect me to make a pie without it?"

"Don't know!" At the word pie, Tiger wagged his tail. "You know where it is ?" Tiger with puckish eyes whimpered. "Come on boy, show us." said Paddy.

"Or you won't have any pie if we don't find it," added Tara.

Tiger hesitated and then dashed to the garden. There, in the middle of the mauled carrot bed, Tiger dug a big hole as fast as he could. He threw out earth and carrots all around. Triumphantly, he brought out the rolling pin.

Tara arrived screaming, "Oh, no! It was you who messed up my garden ! Bad boy!!"

Tiger was expecting congratulations and reward. His eyes went blank and he dropped the rolling pin. What was the matter? He had found it! Tiger watched Tara pick up the rolling pin, with fire in her eyes. Then, it dawned on him what her intention was. Tail between his legs, he scooted away, Tara went after him with the menacing weapon in her hand. Terrified, he just had time to dive under the donkey's cart. Paddy, tears in his eyes, almost choking, bent in two, slapped his legs laughing.

"Don't laugh, Patrick!" Tara said angrily. She went away, holding the rolling pin menacingly above her head. Paddy crawled under the donkey's cart with Tiger.

"Wow. You really goofed! You won't have any pie tonight, if there is any! Come on." Tiger fearfully looked around from underneath the cart.

"Come, let's have a run on the road with my skateboard."

When they came back home. All was quiet, too quiet. Well, if Tara made pie, none was served that evening. Paddy, his homework done said a timid, "Goodnight, Mom," and prudently walked upstairs, mumbling, "Better not rock the boat." Tiger had already crept into the safe haven of Paddy's room and greeted him with a shy thump, thump of his tail on the floor.

Early next morning, Tara was in the garden mending Tiger's damage to the carrot patch. Breakfast had been laid on the table. Paddy ate silently and Tiger, hiding under the table, didn't ask for favors. Paddy grabbed his windbreaker and his school bag and opened the door, followed by a prudent Tiger. "Bye, Mom!"

No response. Tiger wagged his tail, but didn't bark. He chose, at that time, not to be noticed. Paddy grabbed his skateboard and left. Tiger quickly retreated under the donkey cart.

On the road, Paddy stopped to meet a smiling Daryl who was swaying his head to the sound of his Walkman.

"Hi, Daryl. You look very happy."

"Yep. Sophie received a good spanking from Mom. "

"Why?"

"All the cookies mom made for the church's charity lunch disappeared into Sophie's stomach."

"Gosh, she is going to be sick ! Now, what happened last night with your dad?"

"Nothing, I apologized, like you said I should."

"You did ! Good, man! Then what ?"

"Dad said, I accept, but don't try to do that ever again, boy."

"Wonderful ! That's all?"

"Yup."

"All right !" Paddy shook Daryl's hand.

"Dad is not that bad after all."

Paddy jumped off his skateboard and swung it under his arm. They raced each other to school, but Daryl was not a match for Paddy. All day Daryl was in a pleasant mood. A model student, he knew all the answers. In geography, he even knew where the Thames was. The bell rang and Paddy closed his book. Daryl scrambled to go outside, but was stopped by the teacher who congratulated him on his attention in class.

Surprised, Daryl beamed with pride. "Thanks, ma'am."

Paddy seized the opportunity to ask, "Are you coming with me, Daryl?"

"No, thank you, Paddy. You know, I am not the contemplative type. Bye." Daryl waved his hand, plugged the Walkman into his ears, filled his mouth with peanuts, and joined the boys for a game of ball.

"See you tomorrow, Daryl."

"Okey dokey ! "

Paddy swung his board under his arm and went to see his friend. When he arrived, the cliff was deserted. His thoughts drifted to his Dad and how much he missed him. His shoulders slouched and his spirits sank. With a sigh of regret he left. As he reached the pavement he jumped on his skateboard and met Daryl, who had finished his game with the boys. A nasty smirk on his face he asked, "Where are you going so fast man?"

Paddy stopped. "What's the matter, Daryl? Have you lost the game?"

"No one likes me," whined Daryl. "My parents always punish me.""Come on, man, last night your father didn't punish you, did he?"

"Nope, but when I do things, they notice me. My sister is so perfect !"

"No, she is not! Wasn't she punished yesterday?"

"I guess you're right."

"Got to go, bye." Quickly, Paddy gave a kick and hopped on his skateboard. At the gate, Tiger waited.

He entered the house and changed. His mom was busy feeding the chickens. Hurriedly, he went to help and closed the coop for the night, secured the windlass on the well, ran back to the stable, took care of Baltazar, and dashed outside. Tara laughed as she watched him.

"What's the hurry, Paddy?

"Want to talk to Tiger."

Paddy scooted away and sat under the big apple tree talking to his canine friend until Tara called for supper. He jumped to his feet, "Wow! I am starved!"

Dinner over, table cleared, homework finished, Paddy, with Tiger at his feet, curled up in his favorite big chair by the window to read The Never-Ending Story. Through the window, a black human shadow was observing him. Scared, he jumped up, and the shadow vanished.

Next morning, Paddy quickly ate his breakfast, and left.

"Bye, Mom. Bye, Tiger. See you." He met Daryl who was chewing gum and jumping along the road to the sound of some rock music from his Walkman.

"Hi ! Daryl. How about having a run on our skateboards tonight?"

"Good idea."

"Will you come with me to the cliffs after school?"

"What for? I am not cuckoo yet! I leave that to you, dreamer!"

"Maybe one day you will come."

"That will be the day! But who k..n..o..w..s!", He waved his hands in the wind.

It was math day. Paddy liked it and kept away from Daryl who whispered stupid things about the girl in the next row. At last, the bell rang. Paddy grabbed Daryl's arm,

"Have you changed your mind? Are you coming?"

With a grin and puckish eyes Daryl replied, "Why not !" he shoved his Walkman into his school bag.

"Cool, man! All right!" said Paddy in excitement.

They left racing each other. Laughing they dropped their bags and rolled in the dry grass. The squawking seagulls were flying low and Paddy yelled at the daring birds, "Go away! I don't like that, guys! You could take us for a bank and make a deposit on our heads."

Daryl, roaring with laughter said, "After all your visits to their playground, you should be rewarded for being so faithful." Paddy pushed Daryl. "Look, look."

Daryl, flabbergasted, saw the man on the cliff's edge. "Wow! Thought you were pulling my leg. Didn't think he was real !"

"But you saw him, in the cave."

"Sort of. Yes, yes, I did," replied Daryl uneasy, looking at the man standing against the gray sky.

"Good afternoon, Paddy. Good afternoon, Daryl. I am glad you came."

"How did you know we were here? Your back was turned." asked Paddy.

The man walked toward them with long easy strides. "I have a way of knowing things."

"Oh, yes!" Paddy said excitedly. "Tell us about it please?"

The man ignored the plea. He sat, and said, "Give me your hand, Paddy, you, too, Daryl. We will go to my realm."

"No! Thanks!" cried Daryl. Scared out of his wits, he sprang to his feet, and scooted away.

"I thought you said, your friend was brave."

"Yes, he is. Don't understand," mumbled Paddy watching Daryl dashing down the trail. Hesitant, he put his hand into the man's hand.

* * *

In a flash of light, Paddy found himself at the royal court of King Umira, who was happy to see him again. The King introduced Paddy as nephew of the Prince Wizard, Niko, present in the court, and the young human who helped princess Lial defeat the sorcerer Wargo.

Paddy, aghast, whispered to himself, "Then it was not a dream! " He sat quietly on a pillow, feet crossed, elbows on his knobby knees and fists under his chin. Spellbound, his green eyes were set upon the King. The Elf King of light explained about the feud with their neighbours, and enemies, the Dark Elves of the Hazy Forest.

"Domain of the witch," thought Paddy.

"Power is the origin of the feud. Thousands of years ago, one of my ancestors received a gift of great power from his friend, the mighty

35

Fairy of The Twilight. Ever since, the kings of the Dark Elves have craved this power. Two sapphires, eyes of a white onyx swan, are the vessels of this great power. Whoever possesses them can do good, or evil. King Argor, in his own way, is a peaceful King. However, he has a wicked ambitious son, Wargo. Since his last defeat, he burns with the desire to get this power to enhance his own magic. The swan is resting upon the hand of a mermaid statue in the middle of a large pond in our gardens, and is jealously guarded by Zilto, a young dragon, and his friend, Hort the troll."

"A dragon!" Paddy jumped up in fright. Embarrassed by his outburst he shyly resumed his place at the foot of the king.

Chapter 6

"Paddy, you know Wargo, the evil one you fought with the help of my mother, the fairy Zelda" said the king.

Paddy shook his head. Fidgeting on his pillow, bashfully he said, "I am really interested, Sir, but I must return home. Mom is going to worry."

Niko said, "Paddy, time is not the same in the Elfic realm. In earth time, you have been here for a few seconds, even less."

"Oh-o-o!" whispered Paddy.

After supper, a page escorted the young human to his room. Paddy sat in a deep chair pondering what he just learned, about his fight with Wargo. He said, "I know the name. I know the King, too, and Niko the Wizard. Is all this real? Wow, I am all mixed up!"

The castle was soon asleep, but the spirit of adventure got into Paddy. He slid silently out of his room and went exploring the halls lit by gold and crystal candelabras. Here and there stern, spear-toting guards watched him. He continued, curiously peering into sumptuous rooms. His steps took him down the majestic stairs to the gardens, which were lit by iron torches, giving the trees fantastic shapes. The shadows were frightening.

Paddy shivered and froze as, through the power he had received from Woody the Djinn, he saw Wargo creeping into the gentle kingdom, nearing Zilto's and Hort's den. He oozed himself into the pond without a ripple in the water. His long black robe floated around him like a dark cloud as he approached the mermaid. He grasped the little swan and viciously kicked the statue off her pedestal into the water.

Paddy, terrified, fled to the far end of the garden and hid himself in a niche in the stone wall.

Diabolically, the evil one screamed, "King Umira, you are at my mercy. I'll destroy you and your kingdom!" Maleficent words spewed out of his mouth as he held the swan. Vapors and flames engulfed the castle. The country around was charred. With a huge burst of flames and smoke the sorcerer disappeared.

Paddy, had been spared. He looked around, whispering, "Maybe the thick stone wall protected me against the horrible spells. Or Woody's power cloaked me. Now, how am I going to return home? Niko is dead." Tears blurred his vision.

Then, Paddy's power showed him a young elf girl perched in a very high tree in the woods. He felt her terror as she looked at the red sky full of black smoke. She scrambled down. Paddy's heart was choked by her fear. In no time, she reached the edge of the forest.

Paddy cursed Woody for his gift. He had enough of his own fear without sharing others!

Stunned, the girl stopped as she saw the devastated valley. The charred castle, deprived of its beautiful shining windows, blindly looked at the desert realm. She cried and ran calling for her parents. A nasty wind full of dust twirled her hair. Missy dropped in the dirt, crying.

Paddy saw Zilto, the young dragon, and Hort the troll coming out of their cave. Obviously, they had overcome the devilish spell. Fearfully, they looked around and saw the girl sobbing.

"It's Missy," said Hort. They ran to her. Missy got up still crying. "Hort, Zylto! What happened to the palace? Where is everybody?"

"Wargo stole the magic Swan and destroyed everything," replied Hort.

Paddy emerged from the ruins, covered with soot and white dust. Through his tears he saw the three standing in the wind. He ran to them. He was a frightening sight. Tears had made trails on his black face, and his hair was powdered with plaster. Missy, appalled, asked, "Who are you? You are not an elf."

"I came with the Wizard Niko from the earth realm."

"A mortal ! A human! How did you escape the spells?" She asked

"Don't know. Maybe Woody helped." Paddy turned to the troll, "And you. What are you?"

"I am a Troll. My name is Hort." Curiously, he inspected Paddy, who in turn looked at that strange talking, furry thing with flat feet and a long tail ending in a large pom pom. He wore, leather shorts and had a nose as long as a bird's perch. Paddy had never seen such large ears. He mentally compared the Troll's tail with the short one of a French poodle he'd seen in Ireland.

The Troll spoke. "There is a way to restore everything as it was in the past. The sages of the kingdom long ago said that if such a thing were to happen because of evildoing, only a young human boy and a girl, pure in heart would be able to save the Realm." Hort's rounded beady eyes studied Paddy and asked, "Are you that boy? You are human, aren't you?"

"Of course, I am," replied Paddy.

The Troll continued. "The ancients did say, too, that the magic swan would be hidden in an underground chamber, guarded by terrible monsters. If you decide to start the quest, human, Zylto and I will come with you and Missy. The sorcerer may have forgotten the prediction."

"If you think I am the one, I will come," he replied, terrified by the implication.

"What's your name?" asked the Troll.

"Paddy,"

Zylto came to Paddy and thoroughly sniffed him, then he bobbed his long scaly tail on the dirt.

"Zylto approves of your coming," said Hort.

"Really?"

The dragon softly puffed a small cloud of smoke. Paddy said, "We are going to be great friends Zylto."

Hort the Troll took charge of the party, "Let's go to the cave. There are underground passages leading to the edge of the Hazy Forest."

Paddy whispered under his breath, " I am glad the witches won't be there. Maybe Woody will."

"Who is Woody?" asked Missy curiously.

"A friend of mine. I guess, I suppose." replied Paddy.

Like shadows in the wind, protected by a veil of dust and smoke they moved silently to the dark mouth of the cave. The long nose of the Troll sniffed for suspicious odors, then he grabbed a torch secured to the wall. When safely away from the entrance, he lit it and showed the way.

The tunnel floor was full of roots and rocks. Many times Paddy caught Missy to keep her from falling. Suddenly they were assailed by a horrible stink.

"Wow!" said Paddy, pinching his nose.

"Never ventured this far" replied Hort. His long nose quivered.

A growl, enough to chill the blood in their veins, echoed in the tunnel. Two large fluorescent blue eyes shone in the dark. Hort lifted the torch with the heavy mace in his right hand. The light revealed an enormous gray wolf with bared white teeth growling in anger. Terrified, they jumped back.

"Don't be afraid," said a voice from above.

Four frightened pairs of eyes looked up thinking the beast was talking. But no, perched on the neck of the wolf was a tiny man, harboring a grin on his round face. Upon his bright red curly hair bobbed a four-fingered yellow hat. The voice continued, "You are in Rory's den. This is his larder, a place where he stores the Urks he has caught."

Paddy, amazed by the size of the man, mustered a bit of courage and asked, " Who are you?"

"My name is Nam. We little people live by the shore of an underground lake. King Arig heard of your quest and sent me to help. If you children want to, climb onto Rory's back."

"My name is Missy. Thank you, I will." Missy helped by Hort, climbed upon the wolf,

However, Paddy proudly dismissed the offer. "My name is Paddy. Thanks, Nam, I will walk."

The Troll threw his big mace upon his large shoulder, held his torch high and slapped his flat feet on the ground following Paddy and the wolf. Zilto hopped merrily behind.

Missy gratefully buried herself into the thick, warm, fur. Scary noises were all around them. The Troll announced, "In a few hours we will be at the Hazy-Forest, domain of king Argor. His wicked son Wargo ,lives in the mountains."

The cold pierced Paddy's flimsy windbreaker, and his running shoes were soaked by water oozing from the walls. He wished he had dropped his stupid pride and ridden on Rory.

Much later, Nam coaxed the wolf to go faster. " Quick, Rory go! We must be in the forest before daylight." Rory stretched his long legs. Paddy was too tired to run, and the ground was too rough and wet. Exhausted, he fell. From behind, Zylto grabbed his belt and ran with the others. In no time they arrived at the tunnel's end. Rory in a giant leap went through the blocking thorns, as did Hort. Zilto kept his long neck high up, so Paddy wouldn't be hurt. Outside, a fierce wind greeted them. Zilto dropped Paddy to the ground. It was still dark. The air smelled of putrid decay.

"Better come up on Rory's back, boy," said Nam. Paddy didn't refuse this time.

An oppressive silence was about. The ground was pitted with holes full of sharp rocks, and the path was lined with thorns. As they passed near the ruins of the witch's tower, unsettling noises circled around them. Paddy looked at the knoll where he had met Woody.

He whispered, " I am glad to be upon Rory." Tired, he fell asleep in the warm fur. For hours, they tramped through the forest and suddenly faced a deep chasm cutting the path. As Rory stopped, Paddy awoke and jumped off Rory. "Wow! Now what?" he said

Nam thoughtfully replied, "Somewhere, a long bridge guarded by a gigantic spider, crosses over. However, I don't know exactly where."

They resumed their walk along the chasm. Goose bumps all over, Paddy listened to the wind cackling in the branches. After a long wander through briers and thorns, Paddy fell screaming. His legs were ensnared in the deadly rings of a giant snake-like monster with two heads. He struggled bravely to get free. Rory, in a single leap was on the reptile, and his mighty jaws closed on the monster's tail. The snake hissed and let go of Paddy to turn on his aggressor. The wolf, with a powerful swing, threw it into the ravine.

"You are a fierce fighter, boy," said Hort admiringly.

Paddy with chattering teeth, shook his head and mumbled, "No, I am not. Thanks, Rory. "

"Wargo knows we are in the forest," said Nam.

Zylto ravenously started eating anything in sight. They continued for hours with Zylto munching continuously.

The Troll said, "We must have gone the wrong way."

"I don't think so, Hort. See behind the trees?" said Paddy.

A flimsy bridge made of ropes and wood, swayed in the wind across the chasm.

"How are Zylto and Rory going to cross that? " asked Paddy.

Behind, Zylto jumped up and down. Nam turned to look and yelled. "Look! Look at Zylto! See those wings! That's why he was eating so much."

"But how is that going to help us?" asked Missy stupefied.

"Don't you see? He can help us to cross the ravine," replied Paddy inspecting the now huge dragon.

Zylto huffed and puffed showing his sharp teeth, shaking his head up and down. On the other side of the gorge a dark round shadow moved restlessly in its web stretched across from huge trees on each side of the bridge.

" But what about that monster?" Paddy's voice shook .

"Hort, will you help Missy to the ground?" asked Nam.

The little man came down, and stood in front of Rory and made strange sounds with his tongue. Gently the gray wolf took Nam in his jaws, and in one mighty heave threw him into the air toward the other side. As Nam flew, he spun faster and faster and turned into a whirlwind, then into a bolt of fire, which struck right in the middle of the web, turning the spider into a smoking heap. Then, as fast as he had left, he returned to Rory's jaws, where he became Nam again.

To his amazed friends he explained, "In our language, Nam, means bolt of fire. That is what I am!"

Chapter 7

Overwhelmed, Paddy looked at Nam and said, "Zylto can fly Rory across the chasm." Rory growled softly as Zilto grabbed his neck. With a thrust of his powerful hind legs Zylto sprang, his large wings spread.

. Hort, with Nam and Missy upon his shoulders, gingerly walked onto the bridge. Paddy, almost sick with fear, carefully began the crossing. Just as he thought the worst was behind, he heard a dreadful crack. The bridge dropped out from under them and they tumbled down, into thin air. Paddy closed his eyes and screamed.

Zylto, powerful wings flapping in the wind, caught Paddy by his belt in his teeth, and his claws snatched Hort's long hair. The dragon flew to the trail where he gently let them down beside the wolf.

"This is not an accident, but the malicious hand of the sorcerer," said Nam.

The wee man, with Missy, resumed his place on Rory's neck. Paddy shaken up, wordless, walked beside the wolf. With night coming the forest was dark and foreboding. Growling, hissing and other alarming noises surrounded them. Paddy, terrified, clambered onto Zylto's back. Missy hid herself in Rory's thick fur. Hort's powerful hands held firmly to his huge mace. Then, in a clearing a mound of rocks showed a hole like the dark entrance of a cave. Nam whispered, "Wait here. I am small, I won't be noticed. I'll see if it's safe."

Minutes later, Nam returned. "There is nothing that I can see. Hort, Rory, Zylto and I will take turns watching."

They ate and without a word lay down. Paddy fell immediately asleep. Hort took the first guard duty.

Asleep, Paddy in his eye mind saw a monster entering the cave, he woke up screaming, "Look out!" An enormous thing covered with scales, hissing, up upon his hind legs was clawing at Rory whose huge teeth were locked in the neck of the beast. With a terrible clamor it disappeared into the wood. Panting, Rory came to his wee master for well-earned praise and comfort. The Troll quickly grabbed his mace and said, "Better leave. Rory has had enough of a battle."

Missy and Nam went up on the wolf . The night was still deep and cold, and Paddy, in his windbreaker and T-shirt, was freezing. Hours later, morning showed a gloomy face. Icy rain drenched them, drumming their backs. Hort helped Paddy onto Rory, where he buried himself in warm fur. They left the forest to enter a swamp.

Through the veil of rain a deep purple light shone above a high mountain. As Hort looked up suddenly, he disappeared into the snake-infested bog. Bellowing, he resurfaced. Zylto quickly snatched him and tossed him up onto his back. The rain eased up, and Paddy left Rory's warm fur and climbed upon the dragon while Hort jumped down.

After awhile, the large dark mouth of a cave appeared. Zylto froze as he perceived evil with his magic sensors. He huffed and puffed, and out of his powerful lungs came a splendid jet of fire followed by a tremendous explosion. "Wow," said Paddy in amazement.

"That explosion must have been heard by Wargo," said Nam

"You stay here, Zylto, to protect our rear, " said Hort. Zylto lowered his head, grunting unhappily.

"We will be back soon, Zylto," said Paddy. Stiff scared he jumped off.

They entered a large tunnel where a torch was secured to the wall. Hort promptly struck a flint and lit it. Slime dripped from the ceiling. The walls wept icy cold water. They stopped at the bottom of a huge stone stairway winding up in the dark. Rory growled, backed up, showing his teeth.

"You have to climb up, Rory," said Paddy, trying not to show his fear. Bravely he walked in front of the growling wolf.

At the top, they faced an immense hall. The air choked them. Woody appeared to Paddy. "Poison," he said. Quickly the Djinn moved his tiny hand, and he vanished.

"What happened? We can breathe now! " said Nam.

Paddy ignored the question. He didn't want to betray his friend. However, he had saved their lives. Paddy whispered, "Thanks, Woody."

Nam from Rory's back said, "We must move quickly or the spells in this hall will kill us. Let's search for runes. Paddy, look around the floor, I'll look at the walls. "

Paddy searched the ground like a hound dog, nose in the dust. Coughing, he called, "Nam, come and look. There is some funny writing around a flower picture."

The little man climbed down from Rory and, sweeping the dust away, started to translate. " A human child and a little girl with a pure heart are like flowers in a garden. Two shining hearts. Two, touching hands."

"What does it mean?" asked Paddy perplexed.

"I don't know. Children with a pure heart, a human child touching the heart of a flower. That's you, Paddy, the human child, and you, Missy! Hurry! Come down, hold hands and both touch the heart of the flower!" cried Nam.

The little elf knelt beside Paddy, then, both carefully touched the sculpted flower. At that very moment a howl of rage resounded. A stone panel slide open into a room gleaming with shimmering lights, and a sweet voice said, "Welcome, Paddy, human boy. Welcome Missy. Greetings Nam and Hort. I was expecting you."

Aghast, Paddy looked up to see a beautiful Fairy beside an onyx pedestal, upon which rested a little white swan.

"I am the Fairy of The Twilight who, centuries ago, gave the white swan to your king. The terrible spell the sorcerer cast upon the kingdom can be broken only by you, Paddy, a human boy, when you return the swan to the mermaid with Missy's help. Here, you are under my protection and Wargo is powerless. But when you leave this room, you will be on your own. I'll help you as much as I can. However, Paddy, you are the one who must fight Wargo."

The Fairy dropped the swan in a silk bag and tied it with a cord of gold. "I hang this bag around your neck, Paddy. You won't feel the weight. It is now invisible. Only you can bring it back to material matter." She disappeared.

They returned to the hall. Out there, all hell had broken loose. Blazing-eyed monsters of every size and shape waited for them. Rory bared his teeth, Hort's mace flew around him with fury. Terrified the children ran between Hort and Rory.

"You can't escape me. You are at my mercy. I will kill you!" The sorcerer shrieked and laughed. His transparent body floated around, lightning flashed from his hands. Bolts struck the ceiling, the walls and the howling bunch of monsters. The fairy deflected the Sorcerer's attacks. None of his blows were accurate.

They flew down the stairs. Paddy screamed, "Zylto. Stand by. We are coming with the fiends of hell after us!" As they reached the outside, Zylto huffed and puffed and with a powerful jet of fire burned the mob of monsters to cinders. Paddy, more scared than ever, shouted, "Hurry! Wargo can't be far behind,"

Bolts of fire whistled by their ears. Zylto swooped by and scooped the children as they ran. Hort's flat feet slapped the ground, and soon the immediate danger had passed. . They hurried to reach the forest. Of Wargo nothing was heard.

"I wonder what the evil one is up to?" said Nam.

" He must be preparing something big," replied Paddy, quivering at the thought, as smoke began to waft out and choke them. When they came to the gorge it was on fire, a veil of flames rising several meters into the air.

"Wow!" Said Paddy, "Zylto must fly with all of us on board and Rory in his mouth.".

Hort climbed on Zilto's rough hide, then took the children off Rory's back and lent a hand to Nam. Zylto grabbed Rory by the scruff of his neck. Just on principle, the wolf growled. The dragon ignored the protest and hopped and flapped his wings, and they flew quickly up, well above the flames and the forest.

Paddy shivered, feeling Wargo's fury as he witnessed their escape. The Sorcerer's rage was terrible! He sent a storm with lightning, thunder, hail, heavy rain, but with no result. Zylto was now too strong to be stopped.

Their flight was rough. After an almost endless fight with the elements, Paddy could see the devastated kingdom. Dust covered the land and drifted over the ruins.

"What a forbidding sight" said Paddy.

"Not for long friends!" replied Nam.

Paddy knew they were at the end of the quest. Ice ran along his spine. Joylessly he thought about his mom. Niko was dead. How was he to return home?

The storm and Wargo were still after them. Suddenly from behind a dark cloud, a huge red dragon emerged spitting fire.

"Look! Wargo is coming after us!" screamed Paddy.

Zylto quickly dove to the plain and unloaded his passengers. They ran behind a huge boulder, which had not been there a few minutes ago. "The fairy is helping us," shouted Paddy. Hop, and Zylto was in the air again. As he approached the red dragon he mustered all the fire within himself and in one tremendous breath fired at the attacking dragon, hitting his target right in the wide-open gullet. The two fires met and the explosion sent the red dragon flying in pieces. Zylto landed with a flourish and stood with his chest puffed out.

Hort's flat feet thumped the ground. The troll enthusiastically shouted, "Hurrah! Zylto, you are wonderful!"

They walked toward the ruins. It took them almost two hours to get there. Paddy's old fear drummed wildly in his head. Eyes dilated with terror, he looked at Nam, who ignored the plea and said, "You know, children, what to do?"

"Yes," whispered Paddy trembling.

They arrived at what once was the beautiful garden. Violent fear grasped Paddy, and he almost ran away. The wind swirled dust around the ruined pedestal. Paddy's shaking hand reached around his neck for the small bag. A terrible power forced him to strangle himself. The Fairy's gentle voice said, "Missy, touch the bag."

"I don't see it!" she screamed.

'Have faith and you will."

Panic blurred the girl's eyes. Then, suddenly she saw the bag shining on Paddy's chest. Her trembling finger touched it.

"What's the matter?" asked Hort, running to the rescue.

"Wargo is not dead. " cried the boy. Fear in all its horror grasped Paddy. Woody appeared. His slanted eyes were fixed upon the human boy. Gently he said, "Go, Paddy! You can do it! Don't be afraid!"

Chapter 8

Paddy took the swan from the bag and placed it on the ruined pedestal. Magically, the mermaid sprang from the bottom of the pool and placed the swan upon her hand. Water gushed from the opened mouths of the marble dolphins. The castle in all of its magnificence appeared. The young human boy and the Elf girl danced in the water around a beautiful fairy. A strange little fellow with large ears and slanted blue eyes was standing beside Paddy and suddenly vanished.

Missy's parents arrived and snatched her out of the water.

Suddenly darkness covered everything. Vapors of sulfur filled the air, the sun disappeared. A loud cry of rage shook the Realm and lightning scarred the sky. Then, a vast silence fell.

"Wargo is gone for now," said the fairy.

* * *

Atop the cliff an astonished Paddy turned to Niko and asked, "How come I am here? What happened? I was in the Elfic realm. Did I go through the portal ?"

Niko didn't reply, looking faraway across the sea. Paddy continued. "Your name is Niko?"

"Yes, it is."

"Are you really my uncle? How strange. I understand --yet, I don't!" Paddy turned to Niko. He was gone! Troubled and confused, Paddy left mumbling, "Wow! Mom must already be looking for me,"

Paddy grabbed his school bag and ran for home. The garden gate was open and Tiger waited patiently for him.

"Hi, boy! What's up? Where is Mom? " Paddy dashed into the

house. On the table was a note. "I'll be home late. I am going to help Margaret prepare an essay on the legend of The Land of Youth . Your supper's on the table. Don't forget your chores and your homework."

"I won't," he muttered. "How could I?" Quickly, he changed.

As he came out of the chicken-coop, he heard a "psst..psst" from behind the donkey's cart. Curious, he approached slowly. There was Daryl, twisted in a ball behind the wheels.

"What are you doing here? Are you mad! This is a dangerous place to be, man!"

"Shh.. Not so loud!"

"What are you afraid of?"

"My mother is after me.".

"Why? What did you do?"

"Mmm,"

"You better get out of there. If the wind starts blowing, the cart could roll over you!"

Daryl cautiously looked around and crawled out, slithering to the well where he stooped behind,.

"Now tell me!"

"I caught Patou-Minou."

"Your mom's cat ?"

"Yes."

"You know your mom doesn't like you to touch her."

Daryl chuckled. "I tied a small cowbell to her tail. It kept her tail down. Of course the faster she ran, the louder the bell rang. She meowed and meowed. Mom came after me with a heavy yard broom. I barely escaped."

"But you can't hide the rest of your life, " said Paddy, choking with laughter.

Daryl's face lost all its spark. "Maybe her anger will be gone if I wait a little longer."

"No chance! Remember when Tiger dug the carrots from the vegetable garden?"

"Yes, that was so funny!"

"Not for Mom. Adults are not like us," replied Paddy soberly.

Paddy's mom was not back from town, and he shared his supper with Daryl. Chores and homework done, they sat in front of the TV and watched Zorro. The movie over, Paddy sent his friend home and went to bed. That evening, sleep didn't come easily. Too many questions with no answers turned in Paddy's head.

On the road to school next morning, Paddy met Daryl. He was not laughing anymore, neither was he dancing along with his Walkman.

"What happened Daryl ?"

Gloomily, he said, "Mom didn't beat me. I would have preferred that."

"So, what did she do?"

"I won't have any dessert for a month. She knows how to get me!"

"Adults have powerful weapons, man."

The day at school went smoothly. Daryl's spirits had reached the bottom of his stomach. The thought of missing desserts for a month was almost unbearable. The bell rang, the kids noisily jumped from their seats. Paddy dashed out.

"Bye, Daryl!"

"Going to your stupid cliff again to see that stupid man? You're crazy." Daryl shrugged and went home kicking a stone angrily.

When Paddy arrived he sat on the grass. The sea was very calm on the beach below with a soft gentle sound like the breath of a sleeping giant. Paddy muttered, "I wonder who Niko really is? My uncle? No way! Never heard of him."

Niko didn't come. Paddy rose to leave and a movement caught his attention. Scared out of his wits, he saw floating above the rock a human black shadow with flashing red eyes. Hair stood up at the back of his neck and arms. A hissing whisper came from the shadow's mouth, something he didn't understand. Terrified, he bolted down the road followed by the horrid thing. When he got to the gate, it hovered above the hedge laughing, then it vanished. Tiger growled menacingly. Paddy shaking, dropped to the ground beside his bag and grabbed the dog tightly against his chest. Tiger licked his face.

"What was that, Tiger? Once, as I was reading in the living room, I saw it watching me from the window. I am scared." The dog growled angrily.

Paddy went and sat in the orchard with Tiger close to him. Troubled, he thought about the quest. "How come the man Niko was in the Elfic Realm, and so young! Why do I go in and out of the realm? What is that thing that is after me? Is it from the realm?" Paddy was really baffled.

His mom arrived walking briskly, shouting, "Here you are! I went to the neighbours looking for you."

"But I have been here for a while, Mom."

"Betsy talks too much. Hurry! Come and help me. How was your day in school?"

"OK." For sure he was not going to talk about the black shadow. "Mom, may I go play with Daryl after chores?"

"Make certain you are home for supper when I return from town."

"I will." Chores done, Paddy left quickly in case Tara changed her mind and gave him some task to do. Frightened, he looked around for the Black Shadow. When he arrived he called Daryl, who slowly came out from the shed, working on a piece of wood with his knife.

"Ah, that's you," he said still grumpy.

"Let's go playing at the pond," said Paddy.

"Okay! Now you are talking, man." Daryl dropped his piece of wood, folded his knife and promptly shoved it into his jeans pocket

While trampling in the muddy pond, Paddy recounted to Daryl his encounter with the black shadow.

"Wow. This is scary man. What can it be?" he asked curiously.

"Don't know!" Paddy was not yet ready to blab out about his quests in the Realm. They had a marvelous time catching tadpoles. Paddy looked at the pale sun and said, "Must go. I promised Mom that I would be home before her."

"Oh, no, not yet ! We're having so much fun! " Both were covered with mud, and so was Tiger.

"Yes, but I have to clean Tiger and myself. Mom must not see us like that." Daryl shrugged. "Okay, bye! Watch out for the shadow, man."

"Hurry, boy. We had a good time didn't we?" At home Paddy grabbed a large pail of water and carried it into the woodshed to wash Tiger's belly, legs and tail. "Stay still ! Do you think Mom will let you in the house and in my room, muddy and all? No way boy! You were not so fussy in the pond."

Suddenly, Woody appeared at Paddy's side. Startled Paddy stopped, The little Djinn said, "Beware of the black shadow. He wants you and the Green Earth, too. "

Stupefied. Paddy looked at the strange fellow with large pointed bat's ears and slanted blue eyes. Then, having recovered his tongue, Paddy asked, "What? Who wants me? And what for?"

"Wargo." Woody disappeared.

"Now I have hallucinations. Better not say anything to Daryl. But on the other hand, maybe I should. However if I do, I must explained the Elfic realm."

Through with Tiger, Paddy thoughtfully changed the water and gave himself the same treatment. Troubled, he ran with Tiger into the field with Balthazar, who was munching. They got dry quickly and soon were ready to go inside.

"Wargo! Always Wargo!" Fear chewed ferociously at Paddy's stomach. He sat brooding in the dark kitchen. It was night when Tara arrived. He had gone to bed.

Chapter 9

Paddy walked, head down, going to school, pondering his encounter with Woody. He met Daryl with no music.

"What's the matter? You look so grumpy," said Paddy.

"Nothing!" Daryl snapped, "You don't look too good yourself."

"I'm OK. Just worried."

"Worried! What about? The shadow?" Then grumpily he said, "I dipped my sister's ponytail in the fresh bucket of honey on the kitchen table. Dad took off his belt, and let me have it. I am sore all over."

"When are you going to grow up, man?"

"Oh, you!" grumbled Daryl crossly.

The day in school was pretty good. Paddy particularly enjoyed the history class about the invasion of England by the Romans. Daryl, nursing his bruises, had no time to bother anyone.

Paddy found Tiger at the school gate. "How come you are here? Mom won't like it. Come, let's go to the cliffs."

Paddy shivered, closing his windbreaker. Black clouds rolled in the sky. The sea had the colour of lead. Paddy hated the boom of the waves crashing below. His father had been lost at sea on a day like this. He sat fearfully on a rock, his arms around his knees. "I don't think Niko's coming today," he mumbled. Then he heard the voice of his friend.

"Paddy boy, you should go home. A storm is approaching."

"No, not yet. I know the sea, and you still have time to tell me a story. Please?"

"All right, give me your hand. Listen, to the terrible tale of Wargo, master of The Devil's Cauldron.

"Wargo! but I thought he had been crushed! "

"No, not yet."

* * *

A spark went through Paddy's fingers and he found himself once more in the Elfic Realm, at the palace of Queen Yosa, who eyed him in surprise.

Quickly, Paddy said, "Your majesty, I have a message for King Umira from Prince Talua." Paddy looked at the shining bracelet he wore. "Where did this come from." he muttered.

"At the present time, King Umira is not here. The king has just left for the Dwarves kingdom to settle a dispute between them and the Trolls." The queen looked out. Far to the north, a large plume of smoke soiled the sky. She whispered, "The Devil's Cauldron, Wargo's lair, is active this morning."

The Queen's eyes turned to the park below, where the Princess was walking between the old trees. She said to Paddy, "Wargo's marriage proposal to Taima has been refused, and since then the mountain has been boiling and the earth shaking with rage." The Queen sighed.

Thanks to Woody's magic gift, Paddy saw and heard Wargo in his fortress at the top of the Devil's Cauldron, muttering between his clenched teeth, "Taima will be mine! I will trick her." Paddy terrified, watched him disappear.

"Where is he?" Paddy's anxious eyes flitted from tree to tree and to a huge bright bed of zinnias, in the middle of which sat a cute black rabbit. He heard the girl say, "What are you doing here, you little rascal? You are trampling the beautiful flowers! Go! Go away!" She chased him.

Just as it seemed she had cornered the rabbit, he would appear yards away. "How strange," whispered Paddy as he watched the girl Taima laughingly enter into the game going further and further. Suddenly, a red mist covered the girl. Appalled, Paddy saw the rabbit change into the sorcerer. Taima cried out.

With a powerful spell Wargo changed into a huge condor, and turning Taima into a dove, caught her in his strong claws and flew toward his lair.

Paddy screamed, "The Princess! The Sorcerer kidnapped her." The queen run to the balcony and watched the condor flying away. She tried desperately to cast a spell to stop Wargo, but he was much too high.

Paddy's mind's eye saw the sorcerer landing on the tower of his lair, where immediately they reverted to their normal shapes.

The girl was saying, "Lord Wargo! Why? You have scared me so!"

"Don't worry yourself, my dear. Come now."

Paddy, followed them down to a large hall. An old lady with a cruel face entered. The hag cackled, "So, this is the girl," and seized Taima.

"Princess Taima, my sister Argy, Witch of the four winds."

Taima shivered, but curtsied politely.

"Argy will take you to your room."

* * *

Queen Yosa, quickly sent a flying messenger to the king. King Umira flew home at once . There, he found the queen and Paddy. "Hello Paddy, I am glad to see you again."

"Thank you, Sir." Paddy wondered why Niko had sent him into the midst of all these troubles.

"I am going to talk with Wargo. " the king said angrily. "He will return Taima immediately."

Shyly, Paddy asked, "Sir, may I come with you, so I can report to Prince Talua."

"Certainly. Come, boy."

In his private chamber the king went to a desk and moved his hands in front of a sapphire globe to call Wargo. Fascinated, Paddy stood beside the king. The face of the evil one appeared in the globe.

"Good day, King Umira, what can I do for you.?"

The King forced himself to stay civil. "I understand my daughter is visiting you, Lord Wargo."

"I haven't seen her since my last visit."

"We know she is with you," replied the king haughtily.

"Do you doubt my word?" Wargo's eyes flashed with anger.

"Return Taima at once," growled the king, losing his patience.

A loud mocking laugh answered, and the globe turned blue.

Paddy sat motionless. The King with the help of the magic globe, called the young Prince Talua for help. Talua, like his people, had the power of becoming light, almost transparent, so he could fly. Curiously, Paddy looked again at his bracelet.

The prince arrived at once. King Umira explained how to break the spells under which Taima was being held prisoner. Paddy was all ears

"Wargo has a magic Elfic bow in his possession. Centuries ago, the Dark Lord stole it from the Lord of Light. This magic bow, in wicked hands, could be destructive."

"Wargo keeps it in a small room," continued the king, "It is at the top of the north tower, guarded by spells and two gigantic vultures. The only way to destroy the spell is to throw the magic bow into the Devil's Cauldron. That will neutralize the Sorcerer."

Next morning Paddy left with Talua, The prince explained that Paddy's bracelet was magic, with the power to make him fly. A gift to the boy from Niko the Wizard. They didn't fly, as such a long journey would take too much of their strength. Paddy's heart fluttered with fear as he thought about the dangerous quest ahead.

Paddy discovered the perfect place under a big tree for them to sleep. They sat, ate their Elfic biscuits, then rolled up in their capes, and went to sleep. In his sleep, Paddy's power showed him a huge thing watching them from behind a bush. Carefully, it crept to Talua

Paddy woke screaming, "Talua look out!". The beast claws shone in the moonlight like daggers. Its hairy body swayed from left to right as he approached, and its large mouth drooled in anger.

Paddy leapt to his feet. The monster, with a powerful swing of its arm scratched Talua's left leg. At the speed of light the Elf flew into the highest tree. The beast in rage shook it.

Paddy mustered a bit of courage and in a mighty jump landed upon the monster's shoulders, who tried to shake him off, but Paddy held firmly onto the long hair and slowly crawled toward the monstrous head. When he got up between the large ears, he was sweating with fear as he shoved his fingers into the monster's eyes. Howling with pain the beast began to run away. Paddy jumped off.

"You are brave, Paddy," said Talua from his tree.

Shaking like a bowl of jelly, Paddy slumped to the ground.

Talua, slept upon his branch, healing his minor wounds like any elf would. Paddy exhausted, crawled under a bush and fell asleep.

Slowly the sun came up. Talua dropped from the tree, his wound healed. Cheerfully he said, "Well, boy, let's eat and be on our way."

As they reached the edge of the forest, Paddy observed a large open area with small hills and meager bushes, "Looks pretty dangerous to me. No place to hide," he said.

Cautiously, they moved into the short brushes and grass. Then, Paddy cried, "Watch out!" as he saw in his mind the beast oozing between the brushes. Too late! Huge slimy arms with an alligator head quickly seized Talua, squeezing him ferociously. Paddy, terrified, could only watch. It took Talua all of his power to break the slimy grip and crawl away to hide in the brushes. The monster hissed with rage, shuffling around. Just as it found them, they flew up into the air.

Paddy with the help of his magic saw Wargo. His rage shook the Devil's Cauldron. All his plans had been thwarted.

Urgy yelled, "Don't worry, I will stop him!"

Paddy saw the hag rushing to the West tower where a gigantic mill with extremely large sails stood at the top. She moved her bony arms, screaming, "Winds of the North, South, East and West. Blow fiercely."

Terrified, Paddy screamed, "Talua, the Witch of the Four Winds is coming after us!" They were close to the kingdom of the Dwarves, at the foot of the mountains near the Devil's Cauldron.

The attack was terrible. Talua grabbed Paddy's hand and fought with all his power and strength. Exhausted, neither of them could survive much longer. A strong gust from the North Wind threw both to the ground, senseless. A terrible laugh shook the mountains. The witch had won, the wind died down.

The dwarves came out to examine the damage the storm had caused. Paddy, still numb, in his mind, saw the trees uprooted, the roofs of the woodsheds torn apart. Paddy's heart sprung with joy as he heard the donkeys braying from the cool shade of the caves. That day the dwarves had put the animals inside.

Young Zort walked around looking at the desolate site, then, screaming he ran back, "An elf is bleeding to death! A human boy is with him."

Chapter 10

Quickly the dwarves came with two donkey carts and gently put the prince and Paddy on them.

Their dwellings, carved into the rocks, were cheerfully painted with brilliant colors. A system of pipes bored through the rock, brought fresh air in.

For weeks Talua fought death. However, Paddy recovered quickly. As soon as he could, Talua identified himself. King Zarik arrived promptly. "I just heard about your quest, Prince Talua. What can I do to help? We have a large network of tunnels leading to the Devil's Cauldron, unknown to Wargo and his sister. Zort will escort you. He is a very resourceful youngster."

Weeks later, Talua, completely well, said, "Paddy, we are going to resume our journey." They left with Zort. The tunnels were large, with torches in the walls to light their way. Several hours later, they stopped to rest and eat. "From now on," said Zort, "the tunnels are not going to be easy to travel. We will use small torches. I have a few with me."

"Thanks, Zort, but I don't need any. My eyes can see in the dark," replied Talua.

Zort looked at him in surprise and said, "Oh, yes, of course. You are an Elf, but what about the human boy?"

With a sigh of regret, Paddy said, "Yes, I need one please."

It had been centuries since the dwarves last used these passages. They were in bad shape. Strange creatures lived there. Their grunts and whispers scared Paddy stiff who said, "I wonder if these things belong to Wargo?"

Water dripped down the walls. The shaking earth made their gait unsteady and the heat grew intense as they approached the Devil's

Cauldron. Soon the steam coming out of the cracks in the walls soaked them.

Paddy heard something like heavy snoring. "A dragon, Sir," he whispered, as he saw it in his mind.

Talua eyed Paddy and put a finger to his lips. Quickly, the boys blew out their lights and hung tightly onto Talua's coat. They tiptoed forward.

The dragon was enormous and had wakened. It was searching the darkness with flaming green eyes. At the smell of the intruders the monster opened his mouth and shot a powerful jet of flames, showing his terrible fangs. The elf said, "We must go over him. There is no other way.."

"Over him!" whispered Zort, "I don't fly, and I can't see in the dark either!"

"I know," replied Talua. "However, I can't carry you. We would both fall to our death. Paddy and I will distract it. Use that time to get around. The dragon's fire should provide the light you need."

Terrified, Paddy flew round and round with Talua, getting the dragon completely disoriented. It clawed the air trying to catch them and blew fire furiously. Zort didn't waste any time and climbed over the Dragon's tail to get to the other side. Zort reached the safe part of the cave. The dragon became dizzy and, with his eyes still turning round and round in their sockets, collapsed. Quickly, Paddy and Talua landed.

Zort said, "Now, we are not far from the entrance to the sorcerer's lair. I will open the door for you, then leave. I shall seek another tunnel home."

At last the Dwarves' door faced them. It was made of heavy metal engraved with strange runes. Zort concentrated on reading the sacred engraving. With a complicated gesture of his hand, he opened the screeching door. "Here I leave you, Prince Talua. Farewell, human boy."

Talua shook the tiny hand. Paddy, less formal, gave him a big hug, which Zort returned. He then left.

They entered a dark hall. The door closed behind them with the same unnerving noise. Talua searched for Taima's presence.

Paddy whispered, "I can see her, she is alone."

Talua looked at him in surprise. Softly, he said, "Taima, listen carefully. In one hour be at the south door of the castle. Let's go to the tower, Paddy."

Excited, he said, "I see the way to the tower, sir."

"How can you? You are human!"

"I received a magic gift . I can see and hear from afar," replied Paddy proudly.

"All right, then lead on!"

They went up a large flight of poorly lit stairs to a hall where they took another flight of smaller stairs. Paddy said, "I can hear the humming of the magic bow."

They followed the sound, going through halls. Then, they faced a long narrow staircase. They climbed up quickly to arrive on a wide landing with a blank wall, and two large windows. The song of the bow was now loud and clear. On his left, Talua spotted engravings on the wall, and whispered, "Oh, no! Dwarves' Runes!" After a closer examination, he sighed with relief, "Old Elfic runes!"

Talua let his fingers run over certain signs. Slowly a panel opened. In the middle of a small room the bow and a silver arrow lay on a scarlet, velvet rug. Promptly the elf took them. To his surprise the bow felt warm, alive! Suddenly, Talua was prompted to return the bow to the table.

Paddy's green eyes sparkled watching him. Was he going to put it back ? Paddy, muscles taut, was ready to grab Talua's hand. The elf felt Paddy's readiness and said, "Don't worry, Paddy. That was just an instant of weakness, caused by the darker side of the bow."

Bow and arrow in hand, Talua ran to the door and leapt up onto the ledge of the open window, the bow scratching the wall. Paddy followed, wretched with fear. The light sound had roused the birds on a cornice below. With a giant sweep of their wings, the Vultures took flight.

"Fly away boy, hurry! I can't look after you!"

The two of them leaped into the air, but observing the elf going up and down like a yo-yo, Paddy quickly joined Talua and did the same thing. This confused the birds. They became frantic, losing complete control of their flight, finally bumping headlong into each other, they fell to their death into the courtyard below.

"Good show, Paddy! Hurry! I must throw the bow and arrow into the volcano before the Witch and the Sorcerer come after us."

A short distance to their left, the Devil's Cauldron growled fiercely. A red cape flashed in the sky and flew rapidly toward them. The sorcerer attacked the prince with fury. Fire and lightning enflamed the sky. The fight was unequal as Talua had only one hand to defend himself, the other held the bow and arrow.

Paddy cried, "Give me the bow and arrow, Sir. Hurry!"

Paddy didn't wait for an answer but snatched it out of Talua's hand, and flew rapidly away. Now free, Talua attacked the evil one with full force. Paddy, arrived at the edge of the crater and threw the magic weapons in. A gigantic jet of flames engulfed the bow and arrow.

The whole mountain shook. The castle below began to crumble like a deck of cards. Frantic, the sorcerer dropped the fight. Talua, followed by Paddy, flew to the south gate.

As Talua met Taima, he reached into his pocket and took out a bracelet like the one Paddy wore, and said, "This is going to give you the power of flying. Hurry, Taima, put it on! The moment the magic weapons reach the bottom of the Devil's Cauldron the mountain will blow apart, killing all the creatures within. Hurry, Paddy, fly away."

"Who is Paddy?" asked Taima.

"No time to explain. Hurry!"

Talua took Taima's hand and they flew up to join Paddy toward the Dwarves realm.

Darkness fell suddenly. The earth shook with a terrific explosion. The whole sky was red. Two horrible shrieks arose above the sound of the crashing mountain. Wargo and his sister Urgy had been beaten.

Paddy arrived at he dwarves kingdom followed by Talua and

Taima. The people there were delirious with joy. All their fear and terror of the evil ones were gone.

A few months later, both realms rejoiced as the Dwarves helped celebrate the wedding of Prince Talua and Princess Taima. King Zarik's jewelers had made a beautiful tiara of gold, with enormous diamonds, rubies and emeralds. They called it The Tiara of Happiness. They gave it to Taima. For Prince Talua, they made a magic sword as light as the breeze, with the hilt covered in diamonds. They named it The Sword of Faith and Truth. Zort had a special magic ring, with a large ruby the color of blood, made for Paddy his human friend. He called it The Ring of Courage.

In the dwarf kingdom, on winter nights, when the wind howls in the mountains outside, they sit around the fire and tell the tale of how young Zort walked upon the Dragon's tail.

Chapter 11

Back on the green earth, Paddy watched the sky. It had that nasty color he disliked. Curiously, he looked at the beautiful ring on his finger, undeniable proof that, indeed, he had been in the Realm.

Niko beside him said, "Now, go home, the storm is nearing. Don't stop anywhere." For the longest time, Niko looked Tiger in the eyes. The dog barked and wagged his tail. Curiously Paddy asked, "Did you talk to Tiger? He seems to take it seriously.

"I am sure he does."

"See you tomorrow, Paddy. Be careful." Niko was gone.

"I don't understand the way this man moves! Do you, Tiger?" The dog barked.

"You do! You are lucky. Let's go home, boy."

Suddenly, the sky was very dark. Scared, Paddy ran to escape the fury of the elements and didn't notice that his ring flashed bright red. His estimate about the coming storm was wrong. Tiger, behaved most peculiarly by running in circles around his master.

"Are you going to stop that merry-go-round, Tiger? You make me dizzy."

The ring on his finger again flashed red as the dog growled furiously. The whisper of the Black Shadow was in the thunder. Paddy, surrounded by lightning, had blue and red light reflecting on his face and hair. Terrified, screaming, with fear, he bolted down the road. The Black Shadow vanished, laughing. Paddy, shaking all over, whispered, "Could it be Wargo. Tiger? But why in the earth realm? Wow, if he comes here, he will do lots of damage."

As they entered the yard, the thunder boomed louder. Tiger jumped and bolted for the door. Paddy's mom opened it quickly.

"Hurry come inside!" she cried.

Paddy shaken up, needed to talk to his mom. He had to tell her about Niko and the Elfic Realm. Worried he thought," What reaction is Mom going to have when I tell her?" He dashed inside.

Just above them, lightning cracked in the sky. The ruby on Paddy's ring flashed again. Tiger lay trembling under the table. As Tara closed the door, a cataract of rain poured down. Paddy nervously paced around the table, then, mustering his courage he said, "Mom, when I go to the cliffs, I meet a friend. He's an old man who tells me stories from the Elfic Realm and his name is Niko."

"What! You never told me of this man!"

'Why should I have? He is my friend."

"Patrick, I told you many times that I want to know your friends." she said angrily.

"You can meet him tomorrow if you want."

"I certainly will. Now, go and change." Upset, she mumbled, "The Elfic Realm".

Paddy, followed by the trembling Tiger, muttered grumpily as he went to his room. "What's wrong with the two of you? I am glad I didn't say a thing about the whispering shadow and that flashing ring. That would have been something else!"

The storm departed, grumbling away. At the evening table Tara was quiet. Paddy with his nose in his plate asked timidly, "Mom, may I go play with Daryl now that the storm's over?"

"Yes, but don't stay late, and take Tiger with you."

"Of course! Come on, boy, hurry!"

Outside, they whooped and splashed in the puddles left by the storm. When they arrived, Daryl and his sister Sophie were playing in the barn, rolling in the hay. Tiger barked, hearing their laughter.

"Paddy's here. Go to play with your dolls," said Daryl.

"Why?"

"We don't need girls to play with."

"Boys, always boys!" she screamed and stomped away.

"Why is Sophy leaving? She can play with us."

"We don't need her."

"Why not?"

Daryl shrugged. Instead, he pulled Paddy's windbreaker to come inside the barn. They had a terrific game of hide and seek in the hay. Tiger barked his head off, and to their joy, suddenly disappeared, buried in the hay.

"I must go home now, Daryl," shouted Paddy jumping up covered with hay, looking like a scarecrow.

"Not yet! We're having too much fun."

"I promised I wouldn't be late."

"You are no fun. Go then," he said harshly.

"Bye, Daryl. Come on Tiger. See you tomorrow for the picnic." No reply. Daryl brooded in the hay.

During the night, Tiger growled fiercely several times. The next morning a bright sun showed itself. Paddy jumped out of bed. "Hurry, boy! No school today. We are going to have a picnic by the sea with Mom and Daryl."

As they walked out, Paddy noticed strange imprints in the mud near the house. Tiger, the hair up on his spine, sniffed them and growled. Paddy pushed him in the ribs laughing, "Come on, Sherlock Holmes!"

Tara and the boys left the village. Noisily, the two friends chased the dog on the rocky trail. Paddy cried, "Hurry. Mom!"

All morning they played with a soccer ball, with Tiger retrieving it. The lunch was scrumptious, made of their favorite things. They ate sprawled on the warm sand. Tiger, full to the brim, began snoring. Tara's book fell from her lap. The gentle sound of the waves sweeping the sand had lulled her to sleep.

After a while, the boys resumed their game. Paddy was in the water, up to his knees, trying to get near the bobbing ball, when a sudden monstrous wave engulfed him! At that very moment, Tara opened her eyes. Horrified, she jumped to her feet. Tiger, in one mighty leap, was in the sea and with extraordinary strength swam to Paddy, who was going under. The dog grabbed Paddy 's T-shirt and paddled back to shore. Daryl ran to help Tiger pull his friend out of the water. Paddy coughed and spat. Tiger shook himself, splashing everyone, and gave Paddy a slobbery smack .

'"Wow, man, that was a dandy wave," said Daryl slapping Paddy's back, causing him to spit more water.

Tara looked at the sea in astonishment, it had returned to its state of placid calmness. Paddy, forgot that he almost drowned and joyously resumed the game with Daryl and Tiger, chasing after the ball. Tara quickly packed the lunch and they moved up onto the cliffs along a small goat trail.

"Mom, stop! We are far from the rock where I usually meet my friend. We should return to the village and go my way!"

Tara ignored Paddy and continued walking. They arrived where a meager patch of grass grew. Tiger and Daryl lay down and fell asleep. Paddy, too much excited, sat beside his mom. Suddenly a great light shone right in front of Paddy. Niko appeared. Tara, terrified, sprang to her feet.

"Good afternoon, Princess Tara. Hello Paddy."

"Goodness! Who are you? How do you know my name? And I am no Princess."

"This is my friend, Niko, Mom."

"I am Prince Niko, brother of your husband, Prince Ariol."

"But my dad is dead!" shouted Paddy.

"Ariol was no Prince either! What are you talking about?" Tara said angrily.

"You knew that he was an Elf when he married you."

"Dad an elf! This man is crazy," thought Paddy.

"Yes." Tara replied with a smile, "I pretended to believe him. But he never said he was a Prince, and I never told this nonsense to Paddy," she replied indignantly.

Paddy flabbergasted, looked up at Niko and his Mom.

Tara, quite annoyed, said, "Why do you say. he is? Ariol died two years ago at sea."

"No, he is still alive, kept prisoner by the Sorcerer Wargo."

"That's unreal! You take me for a fool?" Tara shouted.

"Wargo! I know that guy. A nasty one," grumbled Paddy shifting his feet.

"I am sorry if it seems to be that way. Listen, please. It was time for our father to pass the scepter to Ariol, my brother, to rule and reign. Father was going to call him back, when the sorcerer captured him upon the sea. Right now, Wargo's plot is to take over the Kingdom with the help of the Urks. We urgently need the return of Ariol to stop him with the power of the Flaming Sword."

"I don't understand! You have the sword. Why don't you free my husband yourself?"

"Unfortunately it's more complex than it sounds. Other than the Prince, who is now prisoner, the legend of the Flaming Sword tells us that only a Human-Elfic child can wield the Sword."

"This is insane! The sorcerer is trying to destroy Paddy," cried Tara who for a split second believed him and was terrified.

"What! " Paddy screamed.

"Yes, Paddy. Do not fear, Princess, the boy is well protected."

"If it hadn't been for Tiger, today he would have been drowned, and stop calling me Princess."

"Yes, but Tiger was there to help. Soon, Paddy will have to come with me into the Elfic Realm. I have prepared the boy through legends to follow me into our Realm." Niko looked Paddy in the eyes and said, "You have met the sorcerer Wargo several times and fought him with courage and determination. Don't forget that you are half Elf. When you are with us, you will discover your powers."

"What! Half Elf! My powers," cried Paddy, glancing at Daryl still asleep.

"I won't let him go," said Tara, "Who tells me all this is true? He is just a boy, and a boy frightened of his own shadow."

"Oh, no, not any more. But I see that you need proof."

"Proof, yes! And more than fairy tales!" she replied angrily.

"Come with me please, you too, Paddy." As the man touched their hands, they crossed the portal. Paddy and Tara, found themselves in a splendid Palace, greeted by the King and the Queen, who repeated to Tara what Niko had already said. Niko, now, to her surprise was a young man.

The king smiled at Paddy and said, "You look just like Ariol when he was your age."

Paddy, in a stupor, looked at the king. It was hard for Paddy to face the incredible reality. Tara agreed to let Paddy go when the time came.

Niko touched Tara and Paddy's hand, and they were back on the cliffs. Daryl and Tiger were still peacefully asleep. Paddy, giddy slumped beside his friend. Daryl woke and with mouth wide opened and rounded eyes said, "But, but this is the man of the cave ! The man who was with us on the cliff a few days ago!"

"I know," replied Paddy chuckling.

"Hello, Daryl," said Niko.

Paddy grinned at Niko, who smiled back, and left in a burst of light.

Tara smiled and said, " I agree, Paddy, he is nice. but elusive."

"Wow! did you see that, man?" said Darryl bemused.

"Mom, do you think we could live in the Elfic realm?"

"Perhaps, Paddy." She laughed.

"Let's go together to the Elfic realm, Mom!"

"Yes, when you find the door, let me know. I will go with you."

"He is crazy ! But I like the idea," said Daryl in good humor.

The three ran home laughing. That evening mother and son joked about the elves and their realm while eating their supper. Tired and happy they went to bed.

* * *

Monday morning Tiger was escorting Paddy to school. Daryl arrived head down, shuffling his feet on the road, with no Walkman plugged into his ears.

" Hi, Daryl. What's the matter? You look as if you had lost your best friend."

"Almost, man."

"You mean Zigar, your pet snake?" Paddy turned around. Walking backward, he watched Daryl. "What happened ?"

"Last night, for fun, I decided to put Zigar under Sophy's pillow."

"What ! Are you crazy man?"

"Yup. When Zigar slithered onto her face, she screamed so much that in a minute the house was in an uproar. Mom made me turn him loose, poor Zigar."

"What about your dad,?"

"He stayed out of the matter. Just looked at me with what I thought, for a moment, was laughter in his eyes."

"So, Zigar's gone. You shouldn't have done that to Sophy. Zigar would still be with you."

"I know, but I would have missed all the fun, too."

Paddy shrugged and turned around. They had arrived at school. Paddy patted Tiger and sent him home. All day Daryl was preoccupied with how to retrieve his pet snake. So, Paddy enjoyed the history class, relating the story of the mighty English pirates working for the Queen of England. The bell rang, the kids packed their bags and ran outside. Paddy put on his windbreaker and tossed his school bag over his shoulder.

Chapter 12

"Bye, Daryl. Wish I could help,"

"Thanks. What a day," Daryl mumbled.

Tiger was at the school gate waiting for Paddy. "Hi, boy! Come, let's go see Niko." Teasingly he said to Tiger. "You are not going to beat me. I can run faster than you! I am an elf! ."

Niko was already on the cliffs, looking at the sea. "Hello, Paddy, hello, Tiger. You look very happy today."

"Yes, I am. I told Tiger that I was an elf and I could outrun him."

Niko smiled. "And did you?

"Tiger is very fast"

"Is it for this reason you are happy ?"

"Not really. I guess it's because Mom is." Pensively Paddy, walked to the edge of the cliff

Niko cried, "Look out !"

Too late! A powerful hand had pushed Paddy in the back. He was falling like a rock ! Paddy closed his eyes. He could hear Tiger howling in despair ! Suddenly, to his amazement he was floating in the air! Cautiously he opened an eye.

"I am flying !" he yelled. "But how?"

Then he saw on his shoulders a gray cape acting like a large wing. It was attached to his wrists and secured around his neck. He whispered, "How did this happen? I didn't have a cape, and even if I did, it wouldn't prevent me from falling. The Elfic cape!" he cried, "I have an Elfic cape! Niko's cape!" He was now soaring upward to where his friend and Tiger were waiting.

"I was flying! I was flying!" he cried excitedly as he set foot on the cliff.

"I know," replied Niko, smiling. "You are an elf, that's why. Sit here, Paddy. First of all, I am not an old man. You saw me young at the palace with your mother. We elves live for thousands of years. The result, when I cross the portal, is that I look very old. In my realm, I am a Prince and a Wizard."

Paddy was boiling with curiosity. He twisted restlessly on the grass.

"All right, all right, settle down. I will take you to my Realm again, and there you will meet Mitsou, Tiger's friend. Then, once more, with her you will go on a quest and fight Wargo, in the tale of The Golden Horn."

"But…but…."

"Listen. Paddy, Mitsou is a cowardly little dog, and learned quickly to be otherwise. Through her example, learn courage. You will need it."

"Why should I ? I am just a kid!"

The elf didn't reply and only looked strangely at Paddy.

"Is Tiger an Elfic dog too?" asked Paddy.

"Yes, he was your father's dog."

"That's why you are so clever!" said Paddy, patting Tiger's head.

The elf smiled and took Paddy's hand. In a flash of light, Paddy went through the portal and found himself in pouring rain at the edge of a forest in his wind breaker, T-shirt and running shoes, standing at the door of a hut. Timidly, he knocked. The door opened.

Paddy, shivering with cold, faced a strong stout man, with long, curly brown hair and a short beard. Quickly. he pulled the boy inside, where a tall young man sat by the fire.

"I am Alcor," said the man. "This is my son, Shuni, and who are you? What are you doing outside in this terrible weather? Well?" Alcor's inquisitive eyes searched Paddy for an answer.

"My uncle Niko sent me to learn the courage I am lacking."

"Niko the Wizard?"

"Yes. You know him?"

"Yes. Don't stand there dripping like a fountain. Shuni, give the boy some clothes."

Slowly, Shuni got up and walked across the small room to a rugged wood chest and took out a brown shirt and pants of heavy woolen cloth, the same as he wore himself. He grabbed his pocketknife and cut the pant leg and shirtsleeves to Paddy's size. Paddy took off his running shoes and socks, set them in front of the fire with his T-shirt and jeans, then put on the warm garments and wrapped himself in a big cape.

"Now sit down by the chimney and be quiet, boy," said Alcor.

The fire crackled and spat. Paddy, grateful for the warmth, crouched silently. The dog came and curled up beside him. Shuni hadn't say a word. Father and son began talking softly. Paddy, with the help of his gift, listened to the conversation concerning Lord Wargo.

"Wargo! Always Wargo," thought Paddy with fear crushing his heart.

That evening the two men were expecting a visit from Ram, king of the Dwarves. Shuni, wanted action, not plotting in the dark like old men. Silently the door opened, letting in a gust of wind and rain.

"Welcome Ram, King of the Golden Mountain," said Alcor standing up.

"Greetings, Alcor, Master of The Blue Forest."

A hooded handsome Dwarf, tall and slender for his race, walked in. His red beard made a dark shadow on his face, where sharp blue eyes shone in the candlelight. A dark red cape, wrapped around his slim shoulders, dripped water on the dirt floor. Quickly, he sat down at the head of the wooden table and invited his hosts to seat themselves.

"Wow, a King!" whispered Paddy.

The King spoke. "My friends, we are here tonight to plan our journey to the Golden Mountain where I ruled and lived. I have been in bondage for years and, with the help of my squire escaped Wargo. It will be an extremely dangerous journey, but a necessary one to gain the freedom of our country." The king continued.

"In one of our caves, deep in the bowels of the earth, near the sacred fire, is a golden horn, made centuries ago at the request of King Or. It is invested with magic powers."

"Magic powers! Wonderful !" Paddy whispered, as he watched the flames. Soon the talking was done. Silently, they waited to depart for the elf realm of King Tariv.

Shuni sat by the fire beside Paddy and Mitsou the dog. As Paddy patted Mitsou, he talked about Tiger and how clever he was, and how he had saved his life in Ireland. Paddy curiously asked Shuni how Mitsou came to his home. The young man scratching Mitsou's ears replied, "Tariv, King of the elves gave her to father, and said, "Alcor, one day this pup will be a wonderful help for you."

Then, in the wee hours of the morning, concealed from their enemies by a dense fog , bundled in their cloaks, Alcor, King Ram, Shuni, and Paddy, followed by Mitsou, left the humble house to meet the king's squire, waiting under a big tree, wrapped in his heavy cape, hood down over his face. After a brief talk, King Ram sent him away.

King Tariv was of the third flying elves realm, the second realm being King Umira and the first realm King Ariol, Paddy's father.

Unmercifully drenched, the party disappeared in the rain, bent against the wind. Paddy was grateful for the warm clothes and the heavy cape. He chuckled at Mitsou, merrily bouncing in the rain, with her long black silky hair dripping. Mud almost covered the white bib and boots. Paddy laughed looking at her unusually long tail hanging like a wet mop. She was a sight!

After traveling through the day in the rain they stopped in a protected area to eat before darkness set in. Young Mitsou was famished. They shared their meager meal with her. Still hungry, she eyed Paddy with interest as he chewed away on a piece of dry meat. "All right, girl, you may have it," he said.

They entered the Blue Forest, which had been Alcor's gentle realm but was now a hostile place with evil power over it , where only creatures of darkness roamed. Alcor said, "I know where we can sleep tonight. Come, Mitsou, be useful. Run ahead and see if the cave is clear."

With worried eyes she looked up at her master. She was not brave, especially at night. With her tail between her legs and a reproachful look in her eyes, she left. A short way down the path, she ran back, terrified and jumped into Alcor's arms, knocking him to the ground. "What's the matter, Mitsou?"

Shuni laughed. "You little chicken!"

Paddy patted her. "Don't worry, Mitsou. My friend Daryl calls me that too,". Little Mitsou whined pitifully.

"Let's see what frightened her so," said Alcor.

Nothing was in sight when they arrived at the cave. Mitsou, forgetting her fear, growled, showing her young white teeth.

Alcor said, "She must see something we don't. Remember, she is an Elfic dog."

King Ram looked at the dog doubtfully.

Paddy, frightened, tired, crawled into a far corner of the cave, and wrapped himself in his heavy cape. Shuni said, "I will take the first watch. Mitsou, you watch with me."

Hair up on her back, Mitsou growled and sat. Shuni's eyes gradually got heavy. Mitsou lay down still rumbling softly. Paddy, in his corner, couldn't sleep. Mitsou growled louder and came to her feet. Paddy, terrified, saw two large red eyes enter the cave, moving slowly toward them. "Look out!" screamed Paddy. The monster hissed savagely.

Mitsou barked back and started turning faster and faster, as if she was winding the spring of a clock, then, with a powerful thrust of her legs flew into the air. Her long tail slashed at the monster's head and killed it.

All this happened so fast, that neither Alcor nor Shuni had even time to move a finger. Paddy and the King were spellbound. Alcor, patting Mitsou, said, "From now on, girl, we will pay attention to your warnings."

"She is incredible," said Paddy.

"Lets see what we have here," said Alcor.

Shuni struck two stones to light a small torch. Nothing was left of the monster except a pile of ashes.

Shuni said, "King Tariv told your father that Mitsou was a great gift. She can feel evil."

The rain had stopped. Morning was coming, damp and cold, and they left the cave. Discouraged, Paddy followed dragging his feet in the mud. Unhappily he mumbled, "Why should I learn courage? I am just a kid, a dud!"

After leaving the forest they came upon a large, dark, deep river. Alcor said, "On the other side we will be safe. However, an extremely strong magic protects the entrance to the elves realm. There is a secret ford where one may cross. I didn't come this way last time, therefore, I don't know where it is."

They searched for hours until Paddy sat to rest. The men continued looking. "I am going to cross here, father," shouted Shuni.

"No! Don't be foolish!" cried Alcor.

"Don't. Shuni, I feel evil there," said Paddy with fear.

Shuni walked into the river. Mitsou pulled at Shuni's leg furiously.

"No! No Shuni !" cried Paddy, terrified.

At that moment, huge tentacles came out and encircled Shuni's waist in a deadly grip. Paddy jumped up and grabbed Shuni's arm and pulled with all his might and Mitsou pulled on his pants, but their combined strength was not enough, and the others were too far away to help.

Paddy fell back as Mitsou let go and started spinning. With her tail, she slashed the tentacles, holding Shuni. By magic, her strength had become tremendous! With her teeth, she pulled him out of the water and gently dropped Shuni on the grass beside Alcor and Ram, who had just arrived.

Chapter 13

Amazed, they looked at Mitsou.

Paddy put a shaking arm around her neck and said to her, "You saved Shuni's life, just as Tiger saved mine."

"I should have listened to you, Mitsou," said Shuni trembling.

"How are we going to cross?" Alcor asked Ram. "The spells are too strong for us."

Mitsou barked and trotted off. She looked behind to see if they were following her. "She is telling us to come," said Paddy dragging his feet, wishing he were home.

Soberly, Alcor said, "And to think that I didn't believe the king when he told me that one day this puppy would help me."

They walked for an hour. Finally, Mitsou stopped and sat waiting for them. Then she stepped into the water.

"No, Mitsou!" cried Paddy.

She barked, encouraging them to follow. Paddy gingerly put a foot in the shallow water. On each side of the narrow ford it was menacingly pitch black.

When they arrived shakily on the other bank, they dropped to the ground. Paddy, fearfully looked at the forbidding black water. His gaze went to the other shore, in time to see several black-hooded creatures enter the water.

"Look, look, they have found the ford!" cried Paddy terrified. Alcor, Shuni and Ram jumped to their feet, as did Paddy who was ready to run as fast as he knew how. Mitsou didn't even move or growl. Indifferently, she continued licking her white paws. Paddy, was completely baffled.

Suddenly from the depths of the river came huge tentacles, which dragged the creatures to their death. Mitsou knew the evil things were doomed.

For the first time since they had left the little house in the forest, everyone relaxed. Mitsou, excited to be home, barked and jumped happily. They walked for several days in this enchanted realm. One morning they entered a beautiful forest where laughter from hidden elf children surprised them. Giggling girls, dressed in long white gowns were perched in the trees, and on higher branches were boys in satin pants and tunics of bright colors.

An escort sent by King Tariv arrived. Paddy's eyes shone as he remembered the marble fountains and fragrant flower gardens he had seen before in other quests. A long flight of white granite steps led them to the terrace where the tall, slim royal couple awaited. They embraced Ram and then addressed the others.

"Welcome Alcor, son of Olcor, Master of the Blue Forest. This young man we presume, is your son, Shuni?" said the king.

"Yes, your Majesty, a fine boy," replied Alcor.

"And who is this child?" asked the Queen smiling at Paddy.

"A human boy from the green earth, nephew of Niko, a friend of mine," replied Alcor.

"You mean Prince Niko, the Wizard, of the first flying elves realm?" asked the King.

"Yes, Sir," answered Alcor.

"I see." The royal couple eyed Paddy curiously.

Paddy felt proud to be called nephew of a prince and a Wizard.

"And you little one, you haven't forgotten who you are," said the King. Mitsou wagged her tail and barked politely. The King smiled and said, "Go to play, girl." In one leap, she was running down the stairs, her long tail flying behind her.

The queen led the way into the gorgeous palace, where a light breeze, coming through the large bay windows, made the crystal chandeliers chime softly, and brought the perfume from the gardens. The King said, "Please, my friends, rest for a while. I will call upon you later."

A young elf escorted King Ram to his chamber, another took the three travelers to their room. Before closing the door he said, "I will come back in one hour and take you to the king, sirs."

Laid out on a chair for Paddy was a traveling Elfic suit, complete with boots and cape. Excitedly, he changed into it.

One hour later, as promised, a gentle bell chimed in the room. The door opened to admit the young elf. After walking through halls illuminated by crystal torches secured to the walls by rings of gold, they arrived at the throne room. Ram, the Dwarves' king, and several notable elves of the court, were waiting. A young elf announced in a clear voice, "His Majesty, the King!" All rose and bowed.

The king smiled and marched to his ornate jade throne decorated with gold flowers. "Please be seated my friends. You know that we are here to talk about the deliverance of the Dwarves Kingdom, and to prevent Wargo Lord of darkness from expanding his evil power into the Green Earth." All nodded. "Wargo's plan is to reduce the dwarves to slavery. Then, he will turn his devilish power onto the Green Earth and crush it." The king continued, "However there is a way to defeat him. Ram, King of the Dwarves will tell us how."

Soberly Ram spoke. "I have already explained to my comrades and friends about the Golden Horn. The enchanted horn is in the possession of Wargo. With it he has vastly increased his power. To regain that horn will be our quest, and not an easy one, by any means."

After a long deliberation they finally decided who was going on the quest. King Tariv said, "You, King Ram. Your kingdom needs you."

"Alcor and Shuni will be the liberators of the Blue Forest. So they must go, as well as young Paddy from the Green Earth. He is indispensable."

Paddy didn't know exactly what all this was about. However, the king had said he was from the Green Earth, and indispensable to the quest. In what way?

Paddy thought, "Wargo, the Black Shadow, comes to the Green Earth after me. Could he stay on earth forever ? The ravages he would make would be terrible! He has to be stopped!"

Paddy heard he King announcing, "Zylf, my daughter has requested the privilege of going with you."

All heads turned as a young elf stood up. Unlike the other elf girls of her age, fifteen, she had short, dark blond, curly hair. She was tall and very slim. She smiled at Shuni and Paddy.

"B-but." Alcor stuttered.

"A girl!" whispered Shuni to his father.

Paddy curiously looked at the young elf girl with her pointed ears.

King Tariv smiled. "Girls in our realm have the same privileges and the same training as boys at the academy. Don't worry yourselves. She won't be a burden to you."

"I hope not," muttered Shuni. "A girl!"

Paddy, surprised, looked at Shuni and thought, "Another Daryl."

Alcor and Ram were not convinced either. Then Shuni came to the conclusion that it would be nice to have someone of his own age in the party. Of course, he had Paddy, but he was younger. Then he gave Zylf a big smile. Curiously, Paddy observed Shuni. Baffled, he shrugged.

"What about Mitsou. Are we to take her with us?" asked Alcor.

"She is your dog, Alcor," answered the King.

"No, I think it will be too long and dangerous a journey. She will stay here with her friends," replied Alcor.

In the morning, when they were ready to leave, Mitsou jumped around barking with excitement.

"Sorry, girl, you must stay here," said Shuni.

Mitsou stopped dancing, sat on her tail and whined sadly, her gentle brown eyes full of reproach.

"Don't cry, Mitsou, we will be back soon," said Paddy.

Zylf arrived dressed, like Paddy, in the uniform of the academy, elf-green pants and dark green tunic made of special material, which kept you either warm or cool when needed. She wore her long gray hooded magic cape and her magic Elfic boots. A little bag hung down from her shoulder. Bow and arrows were in the quiver.

"Hi, Zylf, you look wonderful," grinned Paddy.

Mitsou sadly watched the party leaving and whined miserably. .

Paddy, perplexed, didn't know yet why his uncle, Niko, had sent him here. . "To learn courage," he reminded himself.

They walked north for days through the beautiful Realm. One sunny morning the border was in sight. Since they had to walk through the enchanted gate, the young elf girl took the lead.

Paddy entered the magic portal. Surprisingly weightless, he was in the midst of pale yellow clouds full of sparks, then he appeared on the other side.

No sun! Before Paddy lay a land of rocks, briers, thistles, scrubby bushes and long strings of thorns. Giant potholes pocked the arid ground, like huge chickenpox scars. Paddy looked in disbelief at the incredible sight. A long thorn scratched Zylf's face.

"Ouch! What's that nasty thing?" she said rubbing her bleeding cheek

"Those are thorns. We will find many here," grinned Paddy.

Heavy dark clouds rolled in the sky, and in the distance thunder growled. The temperature dropped, and the men wrapped their big capes tightly around them. Paddy, in his Elfic suit, was nicely warm. Night had come, shrouding everything, and with it came the rain. As the first drops fell they found a large, thick bush to crawl under. The storm showed its nasty temper by suddenly throwing cataracts of icy water upon their fragile refuge. They ate a piece of Elfic biscuit made for travelers, (only a bite carried you for the day), and to save their magic water, drank rainwater. They went to sleep.

They woke in wet, gloomy weather. The small trail was paved with sharp stones, and big roots crept between holes now filled with water. Paddy, head down, heard the sound of horse hooves galloping at a frantic speed.

Terrified, he cried, "Horsemen coming!"

The men threw themselves flat into the muck behind skimpy bushes. Paddy in his haste tripped and fell into a large hole full of water. Shortly, in a cloud of mud and flying rocks, the horsemen went by.

"Wargo's men," whispered Alcor.

Cautiously, the three men came out from behind the bushes. Paddy in his hole heard Shuni ask, "Where are Zylf and Paddy? I am sure the horsemen didn't take them."

A clear voice, said, "Here I am. My cape makes me invisible."

Paddy, unable to get out of the slippery hole, splashed to make himself heard. He couldn't cry out either, as the water would fill his mouth.

Worried, the King asked, "Where is the boy?"

They searched anxiously, while Paddy continued to splash.

"I hear him," Zylf ran and cried, "Over here in a hole. Hurry!"

Quickly, Shuni bent over the pit, grabbed Paddy by the hood of his cape and pulled him out. Paddy shook himself. Thanks to his Elfic suit, he was not wet ,cold, or hurt.

They resumed their walk in the pouring rain. Roots and rocks maliciously twisted Paddy's feet, and the thorns grabbed his cape. At last they reached the end of the tortured land. Ahead, lay a large valley, which Wargo's evil hand had turned into a bog.

The Elfic boots they'd received from the King kept their feet warm and dry. On the horizon, the Golden Mountains, kingdom of the Dwarves, appeared. King Ram said, "Believe me, it will take us days to cross this swamp. Weeks ago, I sent my squire to inform my people of our coming."

Then, Paddy saw something moving in the weeds far behind. In his mind he saw the six horsemen approaching, returning to their master.

Terrified ,Paddy whispered, "Listen."

Ram muttered, "We are doomed, we don't even have a little rock to hide behind."

"Quick, come around me!" said Zylf. She threw her cape over the little group. The cloak magically enlarged and covered them with a shield of invisibility. The horsemen passed like furies.

Paddy noticed closer to them the grass was moving again. They trudged for a long time. Night started, spreading her dark coat. They could not find a dry spot where they could sit or lie, or a tree they might climb. Paddy said in dismay, "We can't stand up all night."

Tired and discouraged, they glanced at each other. Quickly, Zylf threw her magic cloak over them, and they found themselves in a large, perfectly dry tent.

Chapter 14

It seemed a long time since they had slept in a warm place. After eating they rolled in their capes and fell asleep. A small shadow crept into the tent, and left before dawn.

They walked for two more days in the wind and rain. As they approached the mountains, it became bitterly cold. The King said, "Captain Gark, commander of my army, will meet us at Echo Cave."

That day was a forced march. Paddy dragged his feet over the watery ground. Darkness had spread its coat over the weary party when they arrived at Echo Cave. Ram lit a torch found in a small niche in the wall and entered the large cavern. After their meager meal, they settled down for the night.

Shuni said, "I will take the first watch, then Father the second and you King Ram the last, to greet your people when they arrive."

"Thank you," replied the king.

Soundlessly, the small shadow entered and went in a corner.

Paddy's thought turned to the Magic Golden Horn. Who would blow it?

Paddy screamed as he saw in his mind a huge spider-scorpion crawling into the cave. Shuni left his post and came closer to the men. Paddy, terrified, twisted his hands, then a brilliant light flashed out of his fingers, revealing the horrible creature. The men were stunned by Paddy's accomplishment and by what the light revealed.

Paddy forgot all terror! Excited, he screamed, "I am a wizard! See! See!" Elated, he flashed lights at the thing, which slightly backed up. With the help of his new wizardry skill, Paddy tried to destroy it, but his power was not strong enough. The huge body of the spider blocked the entrance of the cave.

"It's impossible to escape," Paddy said in horror.

The spider's fangs dripped in anticipation of a good meal. The clacking claws snapped here and there trying to get at its victims. Paddy ducked, jumping to avoid the deadly snappers. Then, something flew into the air, turning at an extraordinary speed, and snapped off the long sting, the right claw and the left. In the space of seconds, the monster was dead.

"Mitsou!" cried Paddy. "It was you in the grass." Perplexed he said, "But how come I didn't see you? I know! You hid yourself in Elfic power! "

Approvingly, she barked.

The carcass turned to ashes and disappeared.

Aghast, Paddy looked at his luminous fingers, and whispered, "How am I going to get rid of it?" He rubbed his hands. The light vanished.

Soberly, Alcor said,. "You are a wizard, like your uncle Niko. Now go to sleep. I'll take the watch with Mitsou. When your turn comes Ram, I'll wake you."

Paddy, overloaded with excitement, cuddling Mitsou, couldn't sleep. He squeezed her. "I am a wizard! Wow! Neat stuff! I wonder what else can I do?" He chuckled and whispered to Mitsou, " Wait till Daryl hears about it!" He finally fell asleep.

Ram silently came to take the last watch. Early in the morning, the King greeted his men and called Alcor with the rest of the party, "We better move on." Then, he asked the captain in command, " Which road are we using, Captain Gark ?"

"The one with the bridge above the great rift, your majesty."

"Hum, dangerous, very dangerous Gark, but for strategy excellent. He won't be watching that road."

Gark led the way with his men. The dangerous trail crawled up along the mountain's flank, so narrow that you could barely put two feet side by side. For Alcor and Shuni, used to the forest's paths, it was nerve racking. With surprise, Paddy realized that he was not afraid. Then he remembered what Niko had said, "You are an elf, you will discover your power." Wow! he thought, I have already started." Unlike humans, elves are not afraid of heights.

A stone rolled under Shuni's foot. The young man lost his balance and fell into the abyss. Horrified, his friends watched their comrade going to his death. Mitsou wailed with despair. At the speed of an arrow, Zylf jumped into the abyss and passing Shuni she threw her cape onto his back. Suddenly, they floated up toward the shaken group. Paddy helped Shuni onto the trail. Alcor embraced his son. Mitsou patiently awaited her turn. This was no place for exuberance, and she knew it.

"Zylf, I didn't know that you could fly," said Ram.

"Yes, I am a flying elf. Our realm is the second realm, the first realm is ruled by King Ariol, and the third by King Umira."

"Wow! A flying elf! I wish I were one! Ariol! But he's my Dad!" Paddy, puzzled whispered, "Niko said one day I would fly."

Ram gave the signal to resume their journey. Much to Alcor's terror, they climbed higher and higher. For Shuni, every stone became a personal enemy that he watched with each step. After a sharp turn of the trail, they faced the suspended bridge crossing the chasm.

Alcor was speechless. Swallowing hard, he asked, "Must we go on that flimsy piece of rope? I am a brave man, but with things like that, my heart faints."

Paddy, silent, shivered. Ram's men went first and waved them to come. Ram, followed by Paddy and Alcor with his escort, proceeded to cross. The sky became black, the wind started blowing fiercely, howling around them. The bridge swung. Snow and pellets of ice came down. "Hang on tightly to the man in front of you Alcor. You, too, Paddy," shouted Ram.

Paddy, terrified, thought back to another suspended bridge, with him falling down the abyss towards his death and Zilto coming to his rescue. They moved, hunched against the unleashed elements. At last, a hand grabbed Paddy and a strong arm caught Alcor's sleeve and pulled him onto solid ground, where he dropped and kissed the earth.

The King turned to Paddy and said, "You are brave, boy."

Paddy looked at him in surprise. Brave? Him? That was the last thing he expected anyone to say about him!

Then, from the other side, Paddy heard Shuni asking, "How are we going to cross? We can't even see the bridge."

Zylf replied, "Don't worry, we will. Take Mitsou in your arms, stay close beside me. I will put the cape upon us. Here we go!" The cape tightened around them and Paddy watched in amazement as they almost floated across to join the rest of the party.

Aghast, Paddy asked, "Is there anything this cape of yours can't do, Zylf?"

"I don't know. My cape is extremely powerful. It does what I ask it to do."

Paddy's green eyes sparkled as he curiously asked, "Do you mean that all the elves have one of their own?"

"Yes, of course! This is part of our inheritance at birth. It grows with us."

"But what if somebody takes it away from you?" asked Paddy.

"It won't understand any one else, " she replied.

Paddy said. "I see." But he didn't see, he didn't understand all that magic stuff, either.

A heavy snow came down. Ram called his escort, to make sure no one was missing, then said, "The men brought ropes. Let's tie one around our waists to make sure none of us will get lost. Mitsou will be tied up too."

"But we are elves, we can see when you can't," said Zylf.

"I agree, but we can't see you. Therefore, you will be tied, and Mitsou too," replied the King

Quickly, Ram's crew secured the party. The walking conditions were terrible. They fought the blizzard for hours. Discouragement bent their shoulders and then Ram shouted, "We have reached the secret entrance."

An enormous block of black granite emerged from the snow, silent sentry through the ages . The King knelt down and touched the base. The block pivoted, showing a large passageway. Quickly, they entered. Ram turned to face the entrance, whispered a few magic words, and soundlessly it closed. Gark took down a torch held in the wall by an iron ring, struck two rocks together, and lit it.

The King with a sigh said, "At last, I am home!"

Paddy observed the men as they dropped weapons, ropes, and dripping capes to the ground, revealing themselves as being short, strong individuals. Captain Gark was taller than most of the men. All were warmly dressed in heavy brown wool pants with long green wool tunics held by a red leather belt and black leather boots. A thick red woolen helmet covered their heads, with earflaps tied snugly under the chin. Gark wore the same clothes, but a large gold strap crossed his broad chest from shoulder to waist and hooked on a wide gold belt. A formidable ax hanging on the belt denoted his rank. Paddy admired the powerful warrior. Gark signaled his men and took the lead.

They traveled a long way in the well-kept tunnels, climbing several flights of stairs cut in the rock. The party arrived in an extremely vast arena, illuminated by huge flaming torches secured all around the wall by iron rings. When the king appeared in the doorway, loud cheers burst out. With a smile of joy, arms above his head, the King responded.

To his new friends, Ram said, "I leave you in capable hands. You will be escorted to your rooms and later on my attendant will come for you." He departed with his staff.

An elderly dwarf took them through halls lined with magnificent tapestries relating the dwarves history through the ages. Paddy was excited tried to see all of the fabulous frescoes. Zylf was shown to her room, and the two men and Paddy to their quarters, which had a thick rug and heavy tapestries depicting forests and wildlife.

Paddy crawled exhausted upon his bed and fell asleep with Mitsou beside him.

All too soon Paddy awoke with a thought bothering him. Who was to blow the horn ?

.Hours later, with Mitsou, they were officially introduced to the royal court. The King said, "My friends, you have reached the last part of the quest. You will go into the bowels of the earth, to the chamber of the sacred fire, where the Golden-Horn rests. When you have reached the horn, you, Paddy, will sound it."

Aghast, all turned to the boy, who froze on his seat. With wide terrified eyes he looked at the King. Ignoring the surprise he had created, the King continued, "Now, go, I can't tell you any more. Gark will be your guide." They bowed their heads and left.

In the great hall Gark waited for them. Without a word they followed him. Paddy whispered fearfully, "Why me? It can't be me. Why couldn't the King say more? Was he afraid? But of what?" Paddy desperately looked at the others. The carousel of his thoughts turned so wildly that he was almost sick. "The wizard wanted me to learn courage. Is this the test?" Baffled, worried and scared Paddy felt that something had been left unsaid by the King, something dangerous to himself, but what?

They set off again and had traveled a long time in the tunnels when a strange noise came to their attention. Heavy slow steps were coming from the tunnel ahead.

Chapter 15

"A turtle," whispered Paddy seeing the huge gentle beast in his mind. They sat on the ground waiting for the old lady to pass through.

Half an hour later, as they descended deeper into the bowels of the earth, the heat became intense. They were approaching the sacred fire. Alcor's and Shuni's clothing was soaked with perspiration. Paddy and Zylf didn't suffer with their Elfic suits. Mitsou panted a little.

The large cavern was red with the glow of the furnace below and their huge shadows moved on the walls. High jets of lava leaped into the air from the unseen crater. Gark explained, "The sorcerer has the volcano in full blast so no one can get at the Golden-Horn. You can see it shining on the other side of the crater."

"Goodness! How am I going to get it ?" asked Paddy in horror.

"Only a light-footed elf can walk the rod," said Gark . "Look up. See the iron rod passing above the sacred fire? That is the way you must go."

"What! " cried Paddy.

"This is madness!" shouted Alcor.

"It is the only way," replied Gark.

Paddy's green eyes were enlarged with fear, his face was pale with sweat shining on his forehead. "Wow!" he whispered, "This is the test of courage the wizard meant." He shivered. "But I am not an elf," he said.

"Yes, you are, and you know it!" replied Gark. "See, on the side of the wall, small steps lead to the landing where the rod is anchored."

Hopelessly, Paddy looked at his friends and walked away whispering, "Oh, Mom!" Mitsou followed whining. Paddy stopped, and said to her, "All is well, Mitsou, I will do it." Gently, he sent her back to Alcor.

With nerves tensed like strings ready to break, he walked up the stairs, teeth clenched, mumbling, " I have to do it. I must do i. , I can do it." When he reached the small landing, he stretched his arms sideways for balance and slid his feet upon the iron rod. Flames from the pit beneath licked the soles of his boots. The rod glowed dangerously red. Thanks to his Elfic footwear, the heat didn't go through.

Mitsou, nose up, panted heavily. Alcor, Shuni, and Zylf were wet from head to toe. For a split second, Paddy lost his balance! The evil one put terror in his heart and he almost let go.

His friend Woody, the Djinn , suddenly appeared, and grinning at Paddy said, "Look at me. Keep cool man, don't look down, you are almost there," and he was gone.

Green eyes blazing, in determination, Paddy continued. Then jubilantly, Paddy shouted, "I did it ! I did it! Look! I am on the other side,!" Paddy searched for his wee friend and shouted. " Thanks Woody." The Djinn's smiling face appeared. "I knew you could do it."

Zylf flew into Alcor's arms, hugged him and kissed Shuni. She gave a great big smack to Mitsou, who returned the kiss. Gark shook hands energetically with Alcor.

Paddy hesitantly approached the beautiful, ten foot long Golden Horn mounted on a tripod of shining crystal. The long neck, adorned with precious gems, glowed in the light of the fire. For fear of burning himself, Paddy, carefully put a finger on the horn. It was cool ! Then, with all the wind he could find in his exhausted lungs, he blew.

A gorgeous sweet sound filled the cavern. Magically, Paddy was in the sound, floating light as a feather. Then in a splurge of energy, Paddy flew away with the sound into the tunnels, the King's palace, and out into the sky. He was chasing the clouds, purifying the air and bringing back the sunshine. The bog vanished and the wildlife, big and small, appeared in the valley below. Paddy, wrapped in the wonderful sound, turned north toward the forbidden mountain and swirled around several times, feeling the rocks shaking and cracking.

In a terrific jet of fire, the mountain exploded! The sorcerer was gone! Still immersed into the wonderful sound of the horn, Paddy returned to the cave.

The sacred fire, no longer under the control of the sorcerer, had stopped raging. Paddy, with more confidence, walked the rod back to his friends. On their way home, shouts of victory resounded through the tunnels.

Great festivities were given in Paddy's honor in Tariv's court, and, to his confusion, the dwarves and the elves treated him as a hero.

After a few days rest, they left and forded the now peaceful river where the powerful spells had since been removed by King Tariv. Alcor, as in the past, was Master of the Blue Forest with Shuni and Mitsou by his side.

Paddy at the speed of light went through the portal. The familiar boom of the ocean against the cliffs below greeted him. The Wizard was sitting on a rock.

Paddy excitedly turned to him. Talking very fast he said. "Nikko, I walked the rod and blew the horn. Why, did light flash out of my fingers?" His green eyes were full of questions.

But the wizard didn't reply, and commanded instead, "Good. Now go home boy. The storm is coming fast."

Paddy left with Tiger trotting at his heels. Thunder and lightning pursued them all the way home. The black shadow hovered at the garden gate. Paddy jumped back, and his ring flashed red. Tiger growled angrily. The whispering voice said, " I will get you, Prince."

"Leave me alone," shouted Paddy, terrified, running to the house. The first drops came down and the black shadow disappeared. Tara watching from the kitchen window, called, "Hurry up, Paddy, you are going to be drenched."

As soon as the door opened, Tiger dashed inside and dove under the kitchen table. The storm stopped as fast as it had come. However, it rained all night.

* * *

The next morning, the washed country shone and the Green Earth smelled so good. After breakfast Paddy scooted out, " Bye, Mom!"

At the gate, the fiery eyes of the black shadow watched. The ring on Paddy's finger flashed again. The dog growled and showed his teeth. Paddy jumped on his skateboard and bolted down the road with Tiger.

Daryl, on his skateboard arrived behind. "Hey man, don't go so fast! Slow down! Wow, you have a spooky look on your face! Did you see the devil?," Daryl laughed. But when he mentioned the devil, Paddy's ring flashed red again.

"What's that?" Daryl asked curiously.

"What?"

"Your rings flashing weirdly, man. Where did you get it? Let me see." The two of them stopped. Quickly, Daryl grabbed Paddy's hand. "No !" cried Paddy wrestling with his strong friend.

Suddenly both fell into a chasm with swirling waters. Screaming, they seized a rock. A tremendous growling sound came out of the gushing waters, and they saw a long, scaly nose with yellow eyes paddling quickly toward them. Desperately the boys hung on to each other. Then Paddy scratched his ring on the rock. At once they were back on the road, dripping wet.

"What happened?" asked Daryl.

"Don't know. It was scary," replied Paddy looking at the ring .

They raced to school. When they arrived the teacher said, "You are all wet! What happened to you boys?"

"We ran on the stones crossing the creek and fell in, Ma'am," replied Daryl promptly. The girls giggled.

"What creek? Never mind. Sit by the stove, and dry yourselves," she said.

Preoccupied, they sat getting dry. The incident on the road had terrified them. Paddy, absorbed in his thoughts about the Black Shadow, didn't utter a sound. The bell rang and the students dashed to the door. Paddy left, his board under his arm.

Daryl ran after him and grabbing his sleeve, he whispered, "What happened to us, Paddy?"

"Don't know, man."

"You must know! It's your ring!"

"Leave me alone! I am scared too!" Paddy shook his arm and with Tiger on his heels, ran away. When he arrived, Niko was facing the sea.

"Go, home, boy, the weather is becoming ugly."

Paddy started to tell of his encounter with the Black Shadow and what happened with Daryl, but his voice was drowned in a terrible burst of thunder shaking the cliffs. Paddy jumped as his ring flashed. The wind blew furiously. The sea became a sickening yellow and green color. Lightning bolts split the sky, and sudden rain drenched them. Immediately, Niko covered Paddy with his cape. "Go home. Hurry. Run! Hang the cape outside on the doorknob."

Paddy quickly snatched his skateboard and ran home, escorted by Tiger who was going so fast that his belly almost touched the ground. The laughter of the Black Shadow was in the lightning cracking at his heels. At last, the house was in sight. Quickly, Paddy opened the garden gate, dashed for the kitchen door and closed it with a loud bang. Tiger dove under the table

"Ah! Here you are! I was worried.. What's the matter? You are pale."

Paddy chuckled nervously. "I guess I am becoming like Tiger, afraid of the storm." Paddy went to the door, and hung the cape outside.

"Where did that cape come from?"

"Niko lent it to me. He will come and get it later."

"I see," she said.

The storm calmed. Paddy sprang from his chair, opened the door, grabbed the cape and bolted out. A few minutes later he was back almost as fast as he had gone and said, "Went to comfort Balthazar, poor little guy. He was scared, too."

The calm didn't last long. The storm resumed its rage. Supper over and his homework done, Paddy said good night and went upstairs followed by a trembling Tiger. The dog slept on the bed, pressed to the blanket.

In the morning, Paddy ran downstairs and quickly opened the door. The cape was gone. Tara said, "Come to eat, we will be late."

Paddy gobbled his cereal, drank his milk, put on his windbreaker, tossed his bag on his shoulder, grabbed his lunch box, kissed his mother and dashed out.

Several days passed. The weather was terrible and Daryl was sick with a bad cold. Days later Paddy met his friend on the road to school, skipping to the sound of his Walkman.

"Hi, Daryl. I am glad to see you! Are you feeling better?"

" Yup, I'm feeling fine." He gave a sideways look at Paddy's hand. "You know, man, I thought a lot about that ring of yours and about what happened."

"Don't think anything of it and leave me alone!"

"Fine, fine! Hey, you know what? When I was sick I had some desserts. Do you think mom forgot my punishment?"

"Well, I am sure she didn't forget."

In class, Daryl was extremely silent. His day had been ruined by Paddy's answer. Pretending to study, he plunged his nose into his work. Fascinated, Paddy listened to the teacher explaining the law of gravity. When the bell rang, Paddy grabbed his books, shoved them into his shoulder bag, quickly snatched his windbreaker and jumped to the door. Tiger waited outside.

"What are you doing here, boy?" He patted Tiger and shouted "Bye, Daryl."

"Go to your stupid cliffs with your dog," replied Daryl grumpily. "Come with me."

Daryl, snickering, replied, "Nope, I am not crazy. Come on, give me a break! And, I don't want to touch that ring of yours either!" Then wickedly he said, "But who knows. I could do something with it."

When Paddy arrived, the place was deserted. He dropped his school bag and walked to the edge of the cliff and looked down at the waves. Tiger barked angrily. At that instant a powerful hand grabbed Paddy's belt.

Chapter 16

An angry voice shouted, "Don't ever do that! You could fall to your death. Don't you ever listen to Tiger?"

"Yes, I do, but not always. I thought about the last quest, and I imagined that maybe I could fly," said Paddy.

Snapping in irritation, the Wizard replied. "But you cannot! You hear me, boy."

Paddy's green eyes sparkled. "But you said that I am an elf!"

"Yes, you are. But many things have to happen before you can fly. One day you will, I promise. Don't say anything to Daryl about being an elf."

"But why? He is my friend, it would be fun to see his face when I tell him."

"Yes, but Daryl is too mischievous. He could be used by evil powers to hurt you."

"Oh! A few days ago Daryl tried to get my ring. We fought." Then, Paddy described the incident to Niko and asked, "What evil power? The black shadow?"

"What black shadow? You didn't tell me about it!" The wizard's eyes flashed.

"I tried to, but we were interrupted by the storm."

Paddy told what had happened and what the shadow said. Paddy looked at Niko, "I am an elf?"

"Yes, through your father you are a prince, and my nephew."

Stupefied, Paddy repeated, "A prince, and an elf too! Wow! But what about Mom?"

"She will be a queen, and an elf, if she so wishes."

"I can't believe it!"

"Please ask your mother to come with you and Tiger tomorrow,"

"Yes, I will. What a story!"

"Now go home, but watch out. Tiger is an Elfic dog, he can sense evil. Listen to him."

"Wow! An Elfic dog! That's why you are so clever, boy! Dad gave him to me when I was a babe. Then the Black Shadow is evil!"

"Yes, Paddy. It is evil, and the trick with the ring was one of his, with Daryl's help." The elf continued. "Tiger was your father's dog and followed Ariol to the earth realm. Be on guard, Tiger." The dog barked.

On the road home, Paddy pondered Niko's revelations concerning his father. "My father an elf! Niko my uncle!, I must be dreaming !"

Tiger's growling brought him back to reality. A huge green thing with short legs and a large slimy belly oozed onto the road in front of Paddy. It had enormous red eyes. From its horrible mouth, with long hooked fangs, came a sharp tongue flickering in and out menacingly. Paddy darted to the side of the road. The beast's massive head quickly turned. and ferociously it attacked. Unnoticed, Tiger circled behind the monster and in a mighty grip, crushed its neck.

Paddy said, "Thank you, boy." He ran down the road looking back nervously every second. Then his house appeared. Doubling his effort, he arrived. Trembling he pushed the garden gate, closed it, and collapsed on the ground, back against the wood.

A sardonic laugh echoed through the air and whispered, "I will get you." Paddy quivered in terror.

"What's the matter, dear? Are you sick?" Tara asked, running out.

"Tiger saved my life, Mom."

"What do you mean? What happened?"

Paddy recounted the encounter on the road and how Tiger killed it. She knelt before the dog and without a word took him in her arms. Tiger wagged his tail.

"Brave Tiger. Come inside. I will fix you up with a bowl of milk." When he heard milk, Tiger barked. He loved milk.

"Mom, Niko asked you to come with me tomorrow."

"Did he say why?"

"No, only that he has important things to talk about with you and me.

That evening, Daryl visited Paddy , who sat by the window in his favourite chair, a bowl of popcorn on his lap, which he shared with his friend and Tiger as they watched "Voyager" on TV. Then, the door of the house rattled violently. Tiger growled angrily showing his teeth. Paddy's ring flashed. Aghast Daryl asked, "What's wrong with you and this house, man? There is no wind out ! Why does that weird ring of yours always get red?"

Tara entered the living room and said, "It's late, boy, you go home now."

Paddy, in his mind heard a voice whispering to Daryl on his way home, "Get that ring to help me Daryl."

In terror, Paddy jumped up. "Oh, no! the Black Shadow's after Daryl!"

Tara said, "Now, let's go to bed Paddy. The house is well-guarded."

"Guarded! By whom, Mom?" asked Paddy in surprise.

"Go to bed, both of you." She kissed him and patted Tiger.

"Okay, come on, boy." Going upstairs he mumbled. "So many mysteries. Why?"

Tiger slept on Paddy's bed and at times growled menacingly , especially when the house shook and the shutters rattled.

* * *

In the morning Tara said, "You better stay home today. We will go to the cliffs together when I get back from teaching in Donegal."

"But, Mom!"

"Something is getting too close to you. I am glad we are going to see your friend this afternoon."

"All right, but I don't see why. And what thing? And who guards the house anyway!'

Paddy sat by the window and watched his Mom turning the latch of the garden gate and pushing her bike through. She looked back and waved.

Paddy wondered who was after him. Was it the Black Shadow? Did all this have any connection with the Elfic Realm and the event with Daryl and the ring?

For Paddy the day was dull. He surfed the net, watched TV and read a bit. Finally, Tara arrived. Usually fall in Ireland was damp and cold, so she took her shawl, and they left. Daryl joined them on the road .

"Where are you going?" asked Daryl.

"None of your business, man."

"Patrick! What's wrong with you?" said Tara in anger. Suddenly she was unable to move, bound in her shawl!

"Look out !" yelled Daryl, as a seven foot tall monster, partly man partly beast, covered with black shaggy hair, blocked the road. Paddy's ring flashed red The beast with its sharp claws seized Paddy.

Niko arrived on the cliffs and felt evil vibrations. At the speed of light he was on the road. The growls were deafening! Tiger was pulling and biting the monster. Paddy, wet with sweat, was fighting fiercely, when he heard a harsh voice commanding Daryl, "Get the ring," From the corner of his eye, Paddy saw his friend crawling between the monster's legs, and then, he quickly grabbed Paddy's hand with the ring. At that moment both vanished. "Where are we?" asked Paddy in anger. "What did you do that for? Give me back my ring!"

Niko quickly, lifted his right hand. A bolt of lightning came out of his fingers. Then, on the ground was a pile of ashes with Tiger sprawled in the middle of it. And Tara found herself released. She cried "Where are Paddy and Daryl?"

The Wizard made a circle with his hand, and Paddy and Daryl appeared. Paddy with awe asked, "How did you do that? What kind of man are you? I don't understand!". Daryl was round-eyed.

"Did I not tell you I was an elf, from the Elfic Realm,? And a powerful wizard, and your uncle. Don't you remember?."

"A wizard! An elf! Your uncle! I am going insane," mumbled Daryl falling on the grass.

"Give me my ring back," screamed Paddy. Daryl jumped up and bolted down the road.

The wizard looked at Paddy sternly and said, "You lived those quests, boy. They taught you courage."

Paddy sat down in the grass with Tara. The Wizard continued, "Wargo, the sorcerer, knows why your mother came. and he doesn't want you to go to the Elfic Realm. So he sent his evil creatures after you, and Daryl, to help him take you away."

"The Elfic realm!" screamed Paddy. "No! I have had enough! I don't want to play the game any more! Daryl doesn't work with evil! I don't believe you! You are crazy!" Jumping to his feet he continued. "Leave me alone! Leave us alone! I don't want to see you again!" Paddy stumped away. "Enough, is enough! Come. Mom! Daryl was right. This man is insane!"

The Wizard lifted his hand to stop Paddy and continued talking to Tara. "It's imperative that Paddy come with me now. We can't wait any longer. Wargo is getting bolder and we fear for Ariol's life if he destroys Paddy, and he will."

"Ariol, my dad? He is dead! I don't want to go! "

Tara with tears in her eyes said, "Yes, Paddy, your father needs you to free him. If he is not freed, the realm will fall under the evil dominance of Wargo and he will kill your father. You have been with me in the realm. You know it's real. Your father is the rightful heir to the throne."

"Dad? But he is dead! I am all mixed up! How this can be possible? You say you are a powerful wizard, but I am only a boy. You should do it!"

"Unfortunately, I cannot Paddy,"

"WHY? I can't leave mom alone here! You do it, I won't go! Maybe this is just one of your stories." replied Paddy angrily. "I am all mixed up!" He grumbled.

"It is not a story Paddy. Your mother will come later, when she has arranged things and placed the animals."

"I won't go without Tiger! I won't leave Balthazar either!" Paddy felt trapped. Rage lit his green eyes.

"Of course not. Tiger will come with you now."

"I won't abandon Balthazar! And if a monster comes after Mom while she is alone, who will protect her? I won't be there!"

"I promise you, she will be protected, and Balthazar will come with her later on."

Paddy tried several arguments, but each time Niko reassured him. He felt so powerless against the Wizard. The boy was almost crying. "Daryl, I won't see him anymore, " he whimpered under his breath.

"I will be with you soon Paddy. I promise." Tara said.

"Promises, promises! How do I know this is real ? How will you come ? How will you know ? How...." Paddy turned his head to hide his tears. The wizard reassured him,

' "She will come Paddy. Someone will get her when she is ready."

Paddy angrily asked, "But how will you know when she is ready?"

Patiently, he replied. "We have ways of knowing things, Paddy. Remember, one day, you asked me how?"

"Yes, I guess so."

Tara held the boy, took his trembling hand and put it in Niko's. She said, "I love you. Now, go, Paddy."

Meanwhile Daryl had returned to give Paddy his ring and shouted with anger, "Leave him alone! Where are you taking him? Don't let him go ma'am!" Daryl seized Paddy's hand screaming, "You are a wizard, you cou...."

A bright light shone on the road and they were gone. Daryl looked around, stunned. In his hand was Paddy's ring.

* * *

Paddy found himself with Tiger in a beautiful flower garden, a young handsome elf holding his hand. Surprised he looked up and asked, "Where is my old uncle ?"

Niko laughed, "Here I am. I told you, Paddy, that in my realm I was young. You saw me, when once you came with your mother."

"Maybe, but all this is so confusing!"

"I know," replied Niko.

Paddy sighed, "Where is mom?" he asked anxiously .

"She will be here soon Paddy." The boy's face fell.

Then a young elf about Paddy's age dashed down the alley toward them. He cried excitedly, "Hello, cousin Paddy! I am so glad you came. My name is Stoy. Niko is my father, so, you are my cousin," he chuckled.

"How do you know my name?" asked Paddy baffled.

"Simple, each time Father came back from your world, I asked questions about you." He seized Paddy's hand, "Come, I have many interesting things to show you."

"Hold on, Stoy! First thing first, Paddy has to meet his grandparents."

"Can't this wait , Father?"

"No. Paddy will be with you soon. Go now."

Nothing was new for Paddy, the flower gardens, the fountains shooting jets of water in the air the elegant marble palace shining in the sun. He smiled as he remembered having seen them all in his quests.

At the palace, a butler bowed and took them to the king's hall and announced, "Their royal highnesses, Prince Niko and Prince Patrick."

Chapter 17

Paddy looked behind to see whom this Prince Patrick was. No one else was there. He whispered, "It must be me! This is crazy! Me, a royal highness! Daryl would die with laughter." He chuckled quietly and looked down at his hand. "My ring, where is my ring?" Then remembered that Daryl snatched it off his finger. "Little louse!" he whispered.

His expectation of his grandparents was of two elderly personages. But, no! They were young looking people! The King was tall and slim, dressed with a loose gold tunic, held by a belt made of precious stones. His green satin tights disappeared into white leather boots. On his chest a massive gold chain hung, with a large Unicorn cut into a fabulous diamond. Fascinated, Paddy watched the Unicorn flashing in the sun as if alive. The King and Queen laughed. The Queen gently said, "In your world we should be very old people."

Paddy, nodded his head with approval. The Queen was lovely, dressed simply in a shimmering silver gown sprinkled with diamond dust. In her golden hair, which reached her slim waist, shone a sparkling tiara of precious stones. Her large green eyes smiled kindly at the boy. "Come, Paddy, I am your grandmother." Paddy sighed, "I don't think I will ever get used to being a prince. I am just an ordinary boy!"

"Yes, you are a boy. But ordinary, no! No boy is ordinary, but you will get used to being a prince, Paddy. Don't worry about it. Be a boy, be yourself." She turned to Niko and said, "Please, son, take Paddy with you until his mother arrives."

"No, not yet," said the king, as he motioned the boy to sit beside him, and explained the situation concerning Ariol, Paddy's father. All this evil was heavy stuff. Tiger eased himself to the floor beside

Paddy and was not about to leave his master like that, king or no king! Grandfather or not.

"You will have Niko with you. Your uncle is a powerful wizard," said his grandfather.

"I know, I am not really afraid your Majesty...Grandfather."

The King smiled. " Listen, boy, this is your quest. Without you, Paddy, this wouldn't be possible. You belong to the legend of The Flaming Sword. You, Niko, Stoy and Tiger are going to make Elfic history."

"Stoy is coming, too!" asked Paddy excitedly.

"Yes, now listen. The war in the north between the Urks and the Dwarves has been going on for several centuries. The Dwarves are exhausted, almost at the end of their strength. The situation for them is grim. Wargo the sorcerer is at their door and only your father could have helped them, with the Flaming Sword. Wargo captured Ariol from the green Earth, certain that victory would then be his, until he learned of your existence and tried to destroy you,"

King Amah continued . "The Dwarves live quite far away from our Realm. They dwell in the Everlasting Mountains, for centuries envied by the Urks. Our Realm is in The Promised Valley and...."

At this point the story was interrupted, by the arrival of the Dwarves' emissary. Due to a long journey started days ago, the messenger was tired looking and dusty with his boots clogged with mud. He bowed, presenting the message.

The King dismissed the messenger, then sent for his counselors. They talked about the great danger the Dwarves' Kingdom was facing. All agreed that help must be given.

"We will have to get the Flaming Sword sooner than I thought," said King Amah pensively. "Wargo with the help of the Urks, is at the door steps of the Dwarves. The King's message is very clear. Wargo will attack at any moment and hopes to take our Realm right after."

Niko said, "Ariol's mortal son, Prince Patrick, is worthy of wielding the Flaming Sword. I studied the boy through the quests he has lived. I have tested him and many times he has proven his courage."

"Yes, yes. But we have not touched the Flaming Sword for centuries. You will have to deal with the guardian dragon. I know you can, your power is great. When it is neutralized, Paddy may get the Sword. Don't touch it, son! Only the child can! You would be burned to ashes."

"Don't worry, Father. Paddy is a courageous boy."

The King recalled the messenger and said, "Return to Zorga. Tell him we will help. Farewell and Godspeed." The messenger bowed and left.

"Stoy will go with you. It will be a good experience for him. I want you to leave early tomorrow morning. Paddy is courageous, you said? " The king thoughtfully rubbed his chin.

"Yes, Father, he is."

"He will have to be," replied the King.

"Good-bye, Father, until we return."

Silently the King embraced his son and grandson. Paddy, with Tiger trotting at his side, followed Niko.

Next morning the boys and Tiger were ready. Niko came to their door. The elf looked superb, fully dressed with high red boots, brown woolen tights, green pointed hat, and his Elfic gray cape over his shoulders with a quiver full of arrows. He carried the bow in his left hand. The hilt of his Sword showed under his cape. On the right, hung a small bag of survival rations. "Come on, boys, let's go."

Like his cousin, Paddy was proudly equipped with a small sword, a bow and arrows, and, of course, the Elfic cape, red boots, and green pointed hat. They were smaller replicas of the wizard's equipment. Perplexed, Paddy looked at the sword, bow and arrows.

"They are useless to me, Uncle. I don't know how to use them."

"Don't worry, when the time comes, you will,"

"How?"

"They are magic." answered Stoy.

"Oh."

Niko gave a slap on their shoulders, then said, " Move on, guys." The plain was still in shadow, the sun not up yet. However, a clear green ribbon on the horizon announced it would soon be.

"We have to find the Rainbow," said the elf.

"The Rainbow! What for?" asked Paddy.

"To ride it," replied Niko.

"You are joking, Uncle!" said Paddy.

Niko didn't reply. Later, on the shore of a peaceful river, they stopped to eat. After dinner they left the river for the forest. It was almost dark when they arrived at a small village inn, to eat and stay for the night.

"You and Stoy will sleep in my room. It will be safer, said Niko."

During the night Tiger growled. "What's the matter boy?" asked Paddy. Tiptoeing to the door, he quietly cracked it open and peeked outside. A shadow moved away.

The Black Shadow was there . Slowly Paddy closed the door and returned to bed. Next morning, Paddy told the elf about the shadow in the hall.

"Wargo's spy, or even Wargo himself. We will lose him as soon as we are in the rainbow," said Niko.

Early, after breakfast, they left. It had been raining during the night, and the day was bleak. Paddy worried about last night's secret visitor, the Black Shadow. Was it still after him? Tiger walked protectively close to his master. They had reached a valley.

"When are we going to find the rainbow, Uncle?"

"Soon, very soon. It has been raining, boy"

Baffled Paddy looked up. The clouds disappeared, a bright and cheerful sun shone. Excitedly Stoy shook Paddy's sleeve, "Look, Paddy! The rainbow!"

"Wow! It's big and so high. How are we going to climb up there?"

"Come on, boys, you, too, Tiger. Hurry before it disappears!"

Quickly Niko grabbed Paddy's hand but not Stoy's. He was of the realm, as was Tiger , and magic was their world. Paddy suddenly found himself in the midst of beautiful sparkling lights! They were in the rainbow.

"Wow! How did we get here?" yelled Paddy excitedly.

"The Elfic realm is beyond the rainbow, and I am a Wizard,

remember, Paddy?"

"Yes, I know. I wish I were. Are you one, Stoy?"

"I am not," he sighed with regret. "But maybe you are," said Stoy.

"Do you think I could be, Uncle?" asked Paddy, who told him about the lights which came out of his finger in a previous quest.

Niko, busy watching the flow of the rainbow, didn't answer. The colors were fading and the lights dimming. Paddy chuckling said, "Look at Tiger. He is beautiful with all the colors shining on his coat." Tiger barked with appreciation for the compliment.

Stoy with disdain said, "Vain dog."

"All right boys, enough. We have to get off before the lights vanish." As Niko took Paddy's hand, they found themselves on the top of a huge round thing with two horns on the front of its head, crawling in the grass, leaving behind a large shining silvery ribbon.

"Goodness! What's this?" asked Paddy.

"A snail. He is taking us half way down to the dragon's cave." answered Niko.

The snail crawled so slowly that the boys got fidgety and Paddy jumped off with Stoy. Suddenly, they found themselves in a greenish mist.

Too late, Niko cried, "No!"

Growling sounds were all around. Paddy seized his sword as something grabbed his left arm. Quickly, he struck with the blade. A terrible grunt answered and he was free. The greenish mist changed into red. They fell into a deeper pit where the heat was terrible. Long black claws approached Paddy's face. He quickly ducked, then unexpectedly he was back upon the snail. The wizard's eyes flashed with anger.

"I am glad I could stop the snail and cancel the spell you were under!" yelled Niko.

"I am sorry, Uncle. I didn't know." said Paddy.

"Yes, but Stoy should have known better! He is an elf used to living in a realm of magic." Stoy lowered his head. "Sorry, Father."

They spent a day and a night on the snail's back. Exhausted by their fright, the boys slept. Tiger had been quiet. Niko said, "Here boys, eat something. We are almost there."

"I am glad! My legs are killing me! " replied Paddy.

"So are mine," added Stoy, and finally Tiger barked in approval.

"Ah, I see you are still alive," said Paddy patting his dog.

They reached a meadow and the snail stopped. Paddy cautiously waited for the Wizard to get down. As they set foot on the ground the snail vanished and a howling wind shook the trees and thunder growled menacingly. Then cataracts of water came down .

Chapter 18

"Wow!" Paddy's mouth fell wide open. With rounded eyes he looked at Niko.

Stoy chuckled and said, "Not yet used to the realm, cousin?"

They left the meadow, hoods over their faces, heads bent. For several hours the storm raged. Then, suddenly, the wind stopped, and the rain ceased. A beautiful but silent forest was before them. Huge silver spiderwebs hung from the branches. They had to fight fiercely to get past the webs. However, surprisingly enough, the spiders never attacked the travelers.

"May we stop for a while, Uncle?" asked Paddy

"Yes, but I don't like this place," replied Niko.

The boys collapsed on the moss under a big tree full of hanging webs and fell asleep. Paddy's power woke him. Quickly, he jumped to his feet and saw a pair of huge hands brutally parting the bushes. A monstrous furry head appeared. Ferocious eyes looked at Paddy. A large mouth with a double row of teeth, like a shark, opened, emitting a terrible growl.

Tiger attacked like fury, biting a leg. Paddy grabbed the monster's long tail. The beast kicked angrily trying to shake the dog off. With a sweep of its huge paw, the monster knocked Paddy to the ground.

Niko's hand waved and the beast in seconds was reduced to ashes. Tiger growled, sniffed them and lifted his leg. Niko said, "I understand why the spiders didn't assail us. Now they will. Let's move! Fast! Stoy!" the Wizard cried. During that time Stoy had been asleep.

The rattling of the spiders came louder and closer. The spiders, anticipating a good meal, swung in haste from web to web, to reach their victims. The fight against the webs and the spiders became exhausting but they made it to the edge of the horrible forest, only to face rocky soil and pouring rain. Niko said, "Let's find a protected place, boys."

They found a cave. After eating, they rolled into their capes, hoods over their faces and went to sleep.

In the middle of the night, Paddy was wakened by a soft sound of bells. A smiling little fairy, a light in one hand and a tinkling bell in the other, beckoned to him. Daryl, laughing, was dancing with her. Tiger growled, barked and tried to catch the light.

"What are you doing here, Daryl?" asked Paddy surprised..

"Helping the fairy to get you to Wargo." replied Daryl chuckling.

"What! You can't do that, man ! How did you come here anyway?"

"With your ring," Daryl continued laughing.

"Give it back to me!" Paddy grabbed Daryl's hand.

"No way man! I have too much fun. I keep it! Bye!" He vanished.

The tinkling bell woke the wizard. Then he saw Paddy, going away dancing in the night, with Tiger barking angrily. In one leap the wizard had reached the boy. Covering him with his cape he returned to the cave.

"Why did you wake me up, Niko? I was having such a nice dream, and Daryl was there too."

"It was not a dream, Paddy. It was the wicked Fairy Ryia. Her tinkling bell makes you forget everything. This evil fairy is Wargo's accomplice and she was taking you to him, with Daryl's help." Paddy mumbled, "I have my hands full with Wargo and now, just for fun, Daryl is helping him, too."

The morning was cold. A nasty blizzard with pellets of ice had come down from the high mountains during the night. The shivering boys kept their capes snugly around them.

Stoy said, " I hate the cold, Father."

Paddy didn't say a thing. On the coast of Ireland winter was bitterly cold and wet, too. They walked for hours before Niko said, "There it is, on the north side of that mountain. Do you see the cave? "Yes, I do. But how are we going to get there?" asked Paddy.

"By a very small path winding up," replied Niko.

Half frozen, despite their capes, the trio reached the beginning of the trail. Then, Tiger barked furiously, as a large shadow covered Paddy. A gigantic vampire seized him in his claws and flew up. Paddy's free hands, tried piercing the chest with his sword. Hastily, Niko secured his cape and flew after them shouting, "Paddy, tie your cape to your wrists. Be careful when the vampire let's go, it could rip your cape with its claws. Fly freely for few seconds."

"OK!"

Niko, for fear of injuring Paddy, carefully sent lightning bolts. One touched the vampire. Screaming, it let go. The elf rushed to Paddy, seized his hand, and they flew to the cave.

The Wizard said, "The Dragon, lives in a huge cavern far below and goes in and out by another entrance at the back of the mountain,"

They sat behind a big boulder, ate, and immediately after fell asleep. In the morning, it was bitterly cold. During the night, snow had been falling. The howling wind whistled through the cracks of the rock. Tiger's hair stood up on his back and Paddy tried to keep a courageous attitude. Niko said, "We will meet the dragon today and have the Flaming Sword in our hands."

Paddy, terrified, shivered, gritted his teeth. They entered a large tunnel sloping down. It was so dark Paddy couldn't see a thing. Stoy and his father, like all elves, could see. Niko gave Paddy an Elfic stone, which shone with a soft blue light. Stoy said, "I didn't know humans were blind in the darkness."

"I wish I could see, too," sighed Paddy.

"You will. You are an Elf."

The tunnel got narrower. They walked for a long time. Paddy heard a sound like the whistling of a boiling kettle. Scared, he said, "Listen to the breathing of the Dragon."

"Quick, Paddy, put your stone away," whispered Niko.

Paddy put the stone into his pocket and grabbed Niko's cape. Tiger walked beside Paddy. After a while in excitement Paddy grabbed the elf's sleeve, whispering, "I can see in the dark, Uncle Niko!"

"Good, then let go, please."

Paddy, expecting praise from his uncle sighed in disappointment.

117

Stoy chuckled and said, "For us it's not big deal to see in the dark."

"Be silent, boys,"

They arrived at the end of the tunnel overlooking an enormous cavern. Down below the Dragon was asleep, making the hissing boiling noise. Paddy, looking down whispered,

"Wow! He is huge! But he looks so harmless."

"Just wait till he wakes up," replied Niko.

Almost as if he had heard the elf, the dragon looked up with terrible orange eyes. Danger was approaching. He stood upon his powerful hind legs and pawed the air with formidable claws and let out a tremendous roar, accompanied by a terrific jet of flames. Brilliant lights came out of his eyes as he scanned his den from wall to wall. The terrified boys fell flat on their stomachs. The dragon didn't see them. Then, sleepily he crouched down, lay down, closed his eyes, and resumed his nap.

"Wow!" they whispered.

"Paddy, you stay right here. Same for you, Stoy and Tiger."

"Yes, Sir," they agreed.

The elf jumped into the cavern and flew down slowly. The dragon drowsily watched him. The giant beast dozing was no more interested in his visitor than a dog would be in a fly.

When close enough, the Wizard sent bolts of lightning from both hands. The dragon laying roared in anger as he propped himself up. His response was terrible, a powerful jet of fire almost fried the wizard.

However the elf's intention was not to kill the guardian of the Flaming Sword, but cast upon him a long-term sleeping spell. Niko could do it only with the dragon fully awake. The wizard used a ruse he had used several times in similar occasions. Quickly, he flew around the cave in circles. The dragon up on his hind legs, neck stretched, followed Niko's flight and became so dizzy that he lost his balance and fell onto the ground. Immediately the Wizard cast a sleeping spell onto him, and called down to his young comrades.

"But Tiger cannot fly! No, Tiger! Don't ! You'll kill yourself.!" screamed Paddy terrified, closing his eyes behind his hand

Tiger, anxious to go sniffing the dragon, had already jumped. He went down as if on a roller coaster.

Stoy nudged Paddy, laughing. "Look at him," Paddy peeked between his finger. Tiger was on his last roll to the ground. "I thought he would be dead!" Paddy shivered nervously.

Capes tied to their wrists, the boys opened their arms and jumped into the cave. Paddy tiptoed beside the sleeping giant and touched the dangerous snout from which, a few minutes ago, jets of fire had flashed out fiercely. Daringly, he patted the dragon and said, "I have touched a dragon! If only Daryl could see that!"

Niko smiled.

On their left was a very large exit for the dragon and on the right a much smaller one. Paddy, forgetting all prudence and fear, ran into the smaller tunnel, followed by Tiger barking.

"No! Don't !" cried Niko, running after him.

Too late! A net of fire closed on him and Paddy was now in Wargo's hands, bound in ropes of fire, screaming in pain. The quest was in peril of being terminated and Ariol lost forever! The evil one laughed watching him. Paddy in his mind called Woody for help. The little Djinn appeared and attacked the fiery ropes. Paddy was still ensnared screaming. Then, at last, Woody freed Paddy, who, with the Genie's help rejoined Niko and Stoy falling into a very deep shaft. Niko used his power to slow their fall.

Wargo howled in rage. Paddy heard a growling sound and whispered, "Something large is waiting for us below, Uncle."

They landed on the floor of a smaller cave. In a cavity, surrounded by flames, The Flaming Sword shone upon a crystal table.

Fascinated by the sight of the Sword, Paddy forgot the noise he'd heard. A furious grunt brought him back to reality. At the foot of the flames was crouched a huge creature of another age with long hair, teeth and claws like daggers. In a gigantic leap he attacked the human boy. Paddy, quick as an arrow, jumped back.

Niko pushed the boy away. The Elf put into action all his wizardry, tongues of fire, bolts of lightning, ropes of fire. Nothing worked. The thing was a shapeshifter, going from one shape to another. Niko realized that he had to change into something much larger.

Aghast, Paddy watched the elf becoming so big that he almost touched the roof of the cave. The monster tried escaping, but Niko seized the long hair and in a mighty swing threw it against the wall. It fell to the ground like a broken puppet. The wizard returned to his normal size. Niko sat beside Paddy, waiting patiently for the young human to recover his wits.

Paddy noticed the disappearance of the body. "Look Uncle, the carcass is gone," said Paddy.

"Yes, Paddy. The Sorcerer has lost this part of the battle," replied Niko.

"The sword," said Paddy, "Let's get it."

"Remember, Paddy, have no fear. The flames won't burn you as long as you are not scared," said Niko.

Stoy, hand over his mouth, silently watched him go. Paddy's green eyes sparkled, the hot bright flames licked his face.

Chapter 19

Woody, grinning, sprang beside Paddy and said, "Don't hesitate, Paddy! Don't be afraid. Go for it man," and he vanished. Paddy pushed away his terror and went through the flames. Then looking at the blazing flames he realized they had died down! A little bit shaky, Paddy took the sword and turned around. Smiling proudly, he walked to Niko.

Woody's sparkling round eyes appeared. He whispered, "You see, you did it. Be careful, man, you are watched in the dark," and he was gone. Only Paddy could see the djinn.

Niko said, "Hold onto it, Paddy! It is a great privilege to have the Flaming Sword in your hands."

At that moment Daryl emerged from the darkness and ran for the sword. "No!" screamed Paddy. Niko lifted his hand, causing Daryl to freeze, "What's happening?" Aghast, Paddy looked at his friend.

"It is Wargo's doing, with the help of your ring," replied Niko as he moved his hand, sending Daryl back to his world, erasing all memory of the event.

"Wow! Wargo using poor Daryl for his evil plot," said Paddy. Then he gently caressed the beautiful blade and admired the hilt covered with precious stones.

"May I touch it too Father?"

"No, Stoy. It could damage you forever. Only the human/elf boy, his father, or I, for the moment, being protected by Paddy, can touch it. When the quest is over, Paddy and I will return the Sword here, where it belongs."

Regretfully, Paddy gave the sword to Niko. The Wizard reverently took her and kissed the hilt. In response the Sword shone gently.

"Why did you do that uncle? Why did she shine like that?"

"It is a tradition and you must do it too, Paddy. When you are going to use the sword, you make an alliance of truth with her. The kiss is the sign of the alliance, and the glowing, a sign of acceptance."

"I see," replied Paddy soberly.

The wizard gave the sword back to Paddy. The human/elf boy took it and gently kissed the hilt. In response the sword sparked splendid sparks. "Wow!" said Paddy aghast.

"You are fortunate, Paddy. The sword is yours forever. I am just a borrower. In the legend she has never sparkled for any one, till now, for you."

"Really? Wow!" replied Paddy in awe.

Paddy watched the elf taking his own Shining Sword and gently placing it on the now dark crystal table. "Let's go, boys." Tiger jumped around Paddy joyously.

Niko took the Flaming Sword by the hilt and touched the wall. With a scratching noise a panel in the rock slid aside showing a tunnel. They entered and the panel closed. Amazed Paddy asked, "How did you know you had to do that?"

"She is an Elfic blade, and we Elfic Wizards know her secrets."

"I see," replied Paddy, baffled by all this magic. In truth he didn't see anything!

The narrow tunnel went in an almost straight line. At times it turned sharply, only to continue straight again .

"We should be close to King Zorga's Kingdom. This tunnel is a secret passage known long ago to the elven and dwarf kings. However, it is unknown to the present dwarf king, forgotten, lost in time. " Abruptly they faced a wall.

"Now what? " asked Paddy.

Niko took the Flaming Sword by the hilt, and as he touched the wall, another panel opened. They tiptoed into what was obviously a Royal funeral crypt, with many of the tombs bearing images of Kings. Soft light, given off by copper torches spread on the tombs, gave a spooky atmosphere. A set of stairs carved into the rock took them to another level. There, they met three guards ready to attack.

"Peace, gentlemen," said the Wizard. "I am Prince Niko from the

Elfic Realm, escorted by my son, Stoy and my nephew, Prince Patrick." Tiger whimpered gently. "Sorry, boy, I forgot to introduce Tiger the Faithful. We have come to your aid."

The uncertain dwarves consulted each other. Quickly one left. It was not long before he returned escorted by Wurt, the King's counselor. "Excuse us, Prince Niko. We are wary of intruders in this time of great distress for our Kingdom," said the counselor, bowing.

They climbed up several flights of stairs, went through many halls and caves engraved with history and legends. Soon they arrived in front of a splendid door coated with sheet of gold, and the coat of arms of the Royal House. A chamberlain announced stiffly , "Their highnesses from the Elfic Realm are here, escorted by Wurt, counselor of his Majesty."

Tiger unceremoniously went between the chamberlain's legs. The boys held back their laughter.

"Greetings, Prince Niko and you two young Princes. Thank you for coming so soon to our aid. Now, what is that dog doing here, Wurt?"

"My apologies, Sir. Tiger belongs to the quest," said Paddy looking the King squarely in the eyes.

"Welcome Tiger," replied the King.

Boldly Tiger barked back. The King rang a bell, and immediately a page arrived and bowed. "Zar, take our young guests to the play hall."

The Wizard looked at Paddy and said, "Not you, Paddy, stay with us." Tiger didn't move.

"Wurt," said the King, "I will show our guests where we stand strategically. Get ready."

Wurt left and a minutes later with an escort showed the way through tunnels climbing up to a tower built at the top of the mountain. From there, the King had a commanding view of the Urks' army, spread so thickly that the valley was black.

"You see, my friends, without your help, we don't have much hope," said the King sadly.

"With the Flaming Sword and Paddy, the valleys will be soon

cleaned up," the elf replied confidently. Paddy frowned.

That night Paddy pondered and rehearsed the battle plan. Terror sat heavily on his stomach. Was he really the one to do such a gigantic task? But, he had been told that he was the one to rescue his father from Wargo's grip!

Before dawn, Paddy, the Flaming Sword in his hand, left the palace, followed by the wizard and the dwarves army. Through secret tunnels, they reached the edge of the valley.

"Remember, Paddy, be swift in your actions. The Sorcerer is with them. You must not be captured."

"I know." replied Paddy gloomily, ready to take off in the other direction.

The Dwarves wore camouflage of foliage so they wouldn't be given away. The army walked in silence. They had to take the Urks by surprise. Now, they were close enough to see the large tents made of animal hide, which exuded a repugnant odor blended with the strong scent of the Urks. The guards posted around camp after a long watch nodded sleepily upon their spears.

Paddy fought the old fear, which had invaded his mind. Sweat on his brows, he stood paralyzed. "No, I must go," he mumbled. Woody whispered into his ear, "Don't fear, Paddy. The sword is with you, man." Then a shiver ran through his back and he lifted the Flaming Sword above his head. The small shadows moved silently. The stout, hairy Urks, were sprawled on the ground around fires. Their dirty leather clothes stank. Some snored loudly, completely unprepared for battle. The human/elf boy, sword firmly in hand, saw, standing legs apart at the center of the camp, ready to wake the men, a huge Urk dressed in red leather pants, black coat, with a large yellow feathery hat, on his long brown greasy hair. A beard of same color covered his enormous face.

That's the commander, thought Paddy, who quickly took a run at him, jumped camp fires, pushed stupefied Urks around, and attacked their formidable leader. With a sizzling sound, The Flaming Sword destroyed him, and wonder of wonders, at that moment thousands of the Urks burned to the ground. Almost no noise had been made.

Paddy looked bemused at the deserted camp. None had escaped.

"Good work, Paddy," said the Wizard, then to the men, "The battle is not over yet. Paddy and The Flaming Sword must obliterate the other camp in the same way. Let's act swiftly and quietly."

Paddy, his fear gone, excitedly walked beside his uncle. An hour later they reached the camp. A pale sun was up, the Urks were about, eating and fighting among themselves. The dwarves camouflage was efficient. The sword in Paddy's hand flashed in the sun. The wizard lifted his arm above his head and Paddy bolted into the camp, followed by the Dwarves. It was Wargo's camp, and much larger. There were about fifty thousand Urks. With a huge cry, they turned furiously onto the attackers.

The sorcerer left the warmth of his tent and felt, too late, the presence of the Flaming Sword. Paddy guided by The Flaming Sword found the chief commander and struck him down. The Urks burned like straw. Wargo screamed,

"You haven't won yet, young prince! I still have Ariol, your father in my power!"

"Not for long Wargo." shrieked Paddy.

"Well the little Lion roars!" laughed the sorcerer throwing lightning at him, which Paddy deflected with the sword. The raging Sorcerer quickly avoided Niko's counter-blow and threw lightning bolts at him and tried ensnaring Paddy in ropes of fire.

To Paddy's amazement Daryl appeared with the ring flashing on his hand. The boy eased himself behind the sorcerer and tried to strike Wargo with the power he had found in the ring. The evil one felt the danger, and quickly turned around screaming," Don't come again, little brat!" He zapped Daryl, who vanished.

Paddy, petrified by Daryl's disappearance, watched in horror as, Niko and the sorcerer, turned themselves into dragons and sprang into the air. Their cries rang and echoed in the mountains and the valley. Paddy was mesmerized by this colossal battle of another world. Then one of them became much larger. Gigantic flames came out of its terrible jaws and reduced the other to ashes.

In midair Niko, the huge dragon changed into a dove and gently flew down to join the cheering Dwarves. The Wizard had destroyed Wargo! King Zorga knew the battle was over and won by Paddy.

Singing songs of victory, the small army returned to the mountains. Niko and Paddy climbed up the tower to join the king and Wurt. There, Niko said, "Paddy, you have almost reached the end of your quest, the freedom of your father."

"Yes, I know!. Uncle, Daryl was here trying to help me. Wargo zapped him!" With tears in his eyes he said, "I hope Daryl's' not dead !"

The wizard said. "You have the Flaming Sword, Paddy. With her power your father is free. I will turn into a dragon and carry you to the sorcerer's lair. Don't be afraid." said the Wizard.

"I am not," Paddy replied proudly.

King Zorga watched the Wizard leap to the edge of the tower and change into a dragon, Niko whispered magic words and Paddy was on his back as they flew away . The distance was great. Valleys, mighty rivers, mountains, huge forests went by. Then, afar in the mist, Paddy perceived in the clouds the evil mountain. After a while the dragon landed on the highest tower of the sorcerer's lair. Upon the ledge of an open window the dragon returned to his Elfic form, with Paddy beside him.

Chapter 20

Inside the tower a huge wildcat, ready to attack, stared at them angrily. The black slit of his green eyes became thinner, his upper lip curled showing long white teeth. Sharp claws came out as he scratched the stone floor, making deep scars. The long tail slashed the air furiously. Both elves jumped into the room.

The cat sprang. The Flaming Sword in Paddy's hand flashed and the cat was no more.

Paddy said, "Now, Uncle, let's see what is on the other side of that well-guarded door." Niko turned the latch.

With great care they entered a hall from which a narrow spiral staircase wound down. It took them a long time to reach the bottom of the dungeon. Water dripped from the walls. Paddy felt his father's presence.

"Go, Paddy. It is your fight, your last battle. You must do it alone! Your father is waiting for you."

Paddy squeezed the sword. At once he felt a burst of courage in his heart. He lifted his head smiling. Now, he knew the sword and he were one.

Screaming his father's name, "Ariol!" he charged into the damp tunnel. He went through walls of flames, veils charged with terrible spells. He sparked from head to toes. Lightning burst from under his feet. He got tangled in ropes and nets of fire and webs trying to strangle him and fought desperately to get free. Nothing could stop him. He broke all the spells he went through! His body was as light as the magic sword. Sinister laughter coming from everywhere escorted him. Quivering with anger inside, he yelled,

"Wherever you are Wargo, you are dead!" Grunts of fury answered him. Paddy chuckled, "Dead! You are dead, monster." More grunts answered, but Paddy continued.

Once more he called. "ARIOL." Then, far away a faint voice called his name. The sword flashed. Paddy ran as never before and arrived in front of a dragon. For one split second he stopped, then, charging furiously, he went through the beast, which exploded in flames and arrived in front of the cell his father was in. With the Flaming Sword he burned the lock and broke his father's chains and shackles. At last he embraced him!

"Hurry, Paddy, this place is going to blow itself to hell," cried Ariol. They ran to where Niko waited for them. The sorcerer's lair shook violently. The quake got stronger and louder. Vapours came out from everywhere, through the cracks in the floor, from the ceiling and the walls. As they arrived, Niko cried, "Hurry! Let's go."

The tremors were getting terrible. They ran up the stairwell, ran through the halls, and arrived at the large window. Niko, in a powerful jump, landed on the windowsill and changed himself into a mighty dragon and caused Paddy and Ariol to be upon his back, then flew away. Far below, the evil mountain exploded and disappeared forever.

At the top of the dwarves tower, Stoy and Tiger, noses up, anxiously looked at the sky. Then Stoy cried, "There is the dragon!" In a majestic landing the dragon touched the ground. The Wizard once more reverted to an elf.

Ariol hugged Paddy proudly and said, "You have shown great courage Paddy." Paddy beamed.

Exuberantly, Tiger jumped around Ariol and licked his hand.

* * *

One evening, Paddy and Niko quietly left the palace to go down to the crypt. Facing the blank wall, Paddy held the Flaming Sword high in front of him. The wall grated open.

As shadows of the past they entered the tunnel and walked for hours in the deepest silence. Then they faced the closed wall of the cave. Paddy once more used The Flaming Sword to open the hidden door. They went to the crystal table where Niko took his Shining Sword.

Niko whispered as he watched Paddy, "The boy has grown up." Paddy reverently kissed the hilt of the Flaming Sword and said, "I thank thee for thy help. Thou art my friend forever."

In answer, the sword sparked brilliantly in his hands. Paddy laid her down on the crystal table and backed away. A second later the Flaming Sword was encircled by fire.

Paddy said, "Good-bye, till we meet again." As a response the flames flared higher.

They left for the guardian's cave, taking this time the proper route, they finally faced the great beast sleeping quietly. Paddy couldn't resist touching him, but this time with a greater courage than a few days ago and said, "Guard well the sword, friend." They backed up, the wizard moved his hand toward the dragon. A terrible roar shook the caves. The Flaming Sword was again well protected. Hours later they reached the cave. Paddy lifted his hand. With a scratching noise the wall opened, showing the way to the Dwarves crypt. "Uncle, how come it opened for me?"

"Here is the answer to your question. You are a Wizard, Paddy, but you have much to learn."

"I am?"

Early in the morning, Paddy opened the door to his room. Dead beat, without a word, he went to bed. Later, Paddy awoke elated and said to Tiger, "Mom should be at grandfather's palace waiting for us."

Under the friendly eyes of the dwarves, the group linked hands. Niko said, "Brother, take Tiger under your free arm, we are leaving."

Tiger didn't even have time to protest. In the blink of an eye, they were magically transported to the palace grounds, the courtyard full of cheering people . The king and the queen, from the marble balcony, with Tara at their side waved happily. A radiant Tara ran down the stairs to fall into Ariol's arms. When she finally embraced Paddy, tears of joy rolled down her cheeks.

Tiger barked, ran out only to return as fast as he had gone, bringing back his little friend. She sat on her tail, staring at them with gentle soft brown eyes.

Niko said to Paddy, "This is Mitsou, Tiger's friend. She was away with Shuni, her master, and they just returned."

"I remember her! " cried Paddy, "She was with me in the quest of the Golden Horn with Shuni !"

Mitsou followed the conversation with great interest.

"She is beautiful, Tiger! I love her," said Paddy.

Mitsou was so happy! She whirled faster and faster. Suddenly the sky burst with beautiful firecrackers. The children, cheered, jumping, with joy.

Paddy. impatient to know everything about his new world, left with Stoy.

* * *

Weeks later, everyone from far and near in the Realm was invited to the crowning of King Ariol and Queen Tara. Then came the day of the ceremony for Queen Tara and Prince Patrick to become Elves. On a beautiful morning the royal party went to the Sacred Grove. Hundreds of young Elves, boys and girls dressed in white played on small harps and sang softly. They encircled the Royal family beautifully dressed in shimmering white tunics. King Ariol, Tara and Paddy stood hand in hand in a circle. Then Woody and Daryl, Paddy's best friends appeared beside Paddy

Niko the Wizard stood high up on a platform holding a dark blue veil. All whispering had stopped, everyone watched. With the gracious gesture of the fisherman throwing his net at sea, Niko threw the veil over the Royal family. Daryl moved back. The blue veil gently fell, sparkling with stars, and a dim light started to glow in the center of the family circle. The light grew becoming a bright flame. The veil was consumed. The crowed cheered ! The flame was still burning very high without heat. Ariol smiling, turned to his wife and son and said, "Now, you are Elves."

Paddy cried, "I am an Elf! Oh, boy! I always wanted to be an elf." His father laughed.

Paddy ran to Daryl crying, "I am so glad you are not dead! You hear that man, I am an elf! I was so afraid you were dead!"

"Nope, your ring, protected me against Wargo. Here you may have it. Its too dangerous to have, man!" Daryl slapped Paddy's back.

"But, without the ring, you cannot come back here!" cried Paddy.

"I know! Bye. See you in the Earth Realm, man."

"Okey, dokey, it's a deal, man."

* * *

Paddy grew up into a strong, young Elf, a wizard like his Uncle Niko. Years have past and when the young elf returns to his beloved cliffs , he meets with Daryl, who is now an old man. Paddy is old, too. Maybe, one day, Daryl will come with Paddy to the Elfic Realm where he would be a boy full of mischief. Paddy, smiling at the thought, departs in a shaft of light. Daryl sadly whispers, "Just like years ago, in the cave of Melmore head, where it all started with Niko the Wizard."